MARC

Bowen Boys
Book 4

By

KATHI S. BARTON

World Castle Publishing, LLC

This is a work of fiction. Names, characters, places, and incidents are products of the author's imagination or are used fictitiously and are not to be construed as real. Any resemblance to actual events, locations, organizations, or person, living or dead, is entirely coincidental.

WCP

World Castle Publishing, LLC
Pensacola, Florida

ISBN: 9781629890289
First Edition World Castle Publishing, LLC November, 11, 2013
http://www.worldcastlepublishing.com

Cover: Karen Fuller
Editor: Eric Johnston

CHAPTER 1

Jonny tried to control her breathing, but terror and running were taking their toll on her. She slid into an opening after slipping into a darkened alley and pressed her body as close to the wall as she could without becoming a part of it. She closed her eyes, not wanting to see if they found her until she heard their footsteps coming closer. She held her breath and let it out slowly, hoping that they wouldn't be able to hear her.

"Jonny, you know that we're going to find you. It's only a matter of time. We both know that." He walked past where she was, and she could almost touch him. "There are things we can do to make this better for you, but running away isn't going to make me want to help you out."

He moved deeper into the alley where she was and then out again. She could see the man he'd had with him when she'd left the house and knew that he would hurt her if given half the chance. She could see them whispering to each other but couldn't hear what they were saying with all the street traffic.

"I'm giving you one more chance before I have to kill that little friend of yours. You know the one I mean, the little girl that comes to visit you sometimes." She didn't move, because she knew that he'd killed her, or had had

Anita killed, yesterday. "What will you do about that? Having her death on your conscience is going to eat at you."

As soon as they moved out, she let out her held breath. She wiped at the tears but didn't move from where she was. She knew that as soon as she did they could catch her. And she'd rather die than go back there.

Anita was dead. When she'd been trying to escape yesterday, she'd been going through one of the offices when she heard her friend talking. It wasn't until Jonny was nearly ready to come into the room that she realized that Anita was being tied to a chair.

"You do this and people are going to know about it. I want you to let me see Jonny right fucking now." Jonny had started into the room, but backed off when she saw the other man in the room too. She backed away to shift when she heard the soft *pop pop* of a gun, then the sound of someone cursing. Jonny looked back into the room. Anita was slumped over in the chair and a second man was being helped to a chair. He appeared to be laughing, but that couldn't be right.

And now here she was in a dark alley without shoes, without money, and with nowhere to go. She wondered if this could get any worse. Probably. It hadn't been an easy life for her thus far, but she hadn't done anything wrong but been born. Closing her eyes, she wanted to call her mom and dad but knew that their phones were tapped and she didn't want them to be hurt again.

The alley was lit when she woke. Still being careful, she listened for any sound that would alert her that Roy and his henchman, Harris Manning, were around. As soon as she stepped out of the alley, she realized that she had no idea where she was.

Two buildings across from her were typical stores, a Walgreens and a video store. She looked at the two buildings she had been hiding near, and one was an empty storefront, the other a business of some sort. She moved along the empty one, looking for a way to get in. In the back she found a basement window and broke it.

She waited over an hour before she slipped inside. She'd learned before that even empty buildings could have alarm systems that would bring the police, and then Roy and his gang. She bent a large piece of metal around the opening she created so that no one else would come in as well. Jonny moved up the stairs and into the main part of the building.

It had been a long while since anyone had been in the place. There were no footprints in the dust on the floor, and cobwebs were in abundance. She avoided this room in favor of finding another set of stairs that led to the upper floors. She found it in a hall far from the front.

The stairs had mouse droppings. She wasn't worried about rodents. Once they realized she was in the building, they'd scatter. She found the second level of the building had a great deal of old office equipment and furniture, and the third one had been used as a sort of storage room for paperwork. Large file cabinets were lined up in neat and sometimes not so neat rows.

The fourth floor had a semi apartment. There was a stove that ran off gas, a refrigerator that was still plugged in but there was no power, and a cabinet filled with more mouse droppings. She found a bucket and some rags under the counter, along with a few outdated cleaning supplies. Moving among the rooms, she found a bathroom with running water, a shower, and toilet. The last room she found empty save the large dresser, which was also empty.

Smiling for the first time in months, she thought she could live here for a little while at least.

Without money she couldn't buy food, but she wasn't stupid either. She went to the front of the upper windows and watched the street below her. She hated to steal, but if she could get a pair of shoes and some toiletries, she could find a job and repay whomever she had to "borrow" from; because that's what it was going to be, borrowing not stealing.

By nightfall she'd cleaned up as best she could. She'd found a few more supplies, such as a broom and dust pan, on the second floor, and had even unearthed a chair that wasn't in too bad of shape among the furniture. On the third floor she'd found a brand new yet very old shower curtain, which she hung with twisty ties she'd found in one of the cabinet drawers.

By the time she decided to go to bed that night, the kitchen was spotless and the room she was in was cleared off all cobwebs and dirt, and she'd even polished the old dresser to a nice shine. Closing her eyes, she felt safer here than she had in a very long time.

When she woke the next time, it took her several seconds to realize she was safe. She calmed her cat down with soothing words and stood up. Looking out the window, she saw a lone car in the lot next to her. Moving to the front of the building, she watched to see how much traffic there was and decided that the few cars that went by were far enough apart that she could do what she needed.

She moved out of the basement window and made sure that she closed the entrance up again. Moving along the back of the buildings, she watched for one that looked to be occupied but empty of people. She found one about three blocks from her new home.

Finding the same kind of low window at the basement, she broke the glass and waited. A cruiser went by once but didn't stop. She waited another twenty minutes and moved into the building. It wasn't until she was inside that she realized that it was an old shop that seemed to deal in used clothing. Excited but careful, she shifted to cat and moved through the showroom floor to the offices in the back, thinking that the black cat would be hard to see. She looked around for any sort of video equipment and even searched through the mess on the desk. She decided that anyone this messy and unorganized wouldn't have a clue what they had on the floor. She went to the bags of stuff the person had tossed on the floor first. Shifting back to herself, she looked around at the piles of things.

She decided this was to be thrown out. There was nothing worth saving even if she was going to wear it around her new apartment. Zippers had been removed and buttons taken off. She did find a pair of tennis shoes that fit her but they had no laces. Even so, she put them in a pile she was going to take with her. Next, she moved to the floor. She found out why the zippers had been removed before being tossed out.

The owner was selling them as "vintage." She knew what the word meant but she doubted that the owner did. They were used, not old. She moved to a section someone had marked as "the ladies" and looked for something suitable to wear. She flinched every time someone's lights shined in the front window.

She had five blouses, three pairs of pants, and a pair of shoes. She found a nice sweater and had a jacket but couldn't make the zipper work well and put it back, wondering if it would end up in the bag of trash and the zipper in his vintage pile. There were panties and bras as well, but she refused to think what sort of person would wear used under things. Moving to the back of the store where the basement access was, she looked at the cash register again.

She needed money. But did she need it more than the person selling these things? Jonny looked around the store and decided that the owner needed it more. Going out before she convinced herself that she did need it, she slipped out of the basement encasement. Making sure that the window wouldn't let anyone else in, she stuffed all her things into a bag she'd taken as well and made her way back to the apartment.

There was a woman in the alley this time. She was moving along the lone car as if she were drunk. Jonny waited until she was out of sight before she moved to the window again and inside. She was exhausted and moved straight to her room. Laying down, she got back up and hung all her clothes in the bare closet with some of the hangers she'd found, and then lay back down. There was something very personal about having her own clothes in her own closet. She was asleep within minutes.

~~~

"Do we know what killed her?" Marc looked at his team when no one answered. "We have to have something on this. The murder happened three days ago."

"The guy I have at the station says it was a wild dog. I don't know, he seemed fascinated with the idea that there might be a wild dog on the loose." Dewey Ortiz shifted in his chair and handed him a picture. "I don't think a dog would have done that one, boss. More likely a man with a rake."

Marc looked at the picture carefully. He was right, it looked like a rake. He looked up at Mia when she walked
~~~

in. She didn't look pleased, which, looking at her in the later part of her pregnancy, he could see why. She was carrying twins and looked like she needed a hoist to help her move.

"Hey girl," he grinned at her. "You look very fetching in that blouse. What have you got for me?"

"I have the autopsy report on Miss Rutledge. According to the report, she was shot once in the back of the head, and then her body was mutilated with a sharp instrument, probably a rake or some other evenly spaced equipment."

He grinned at Dewey when he yelled, then looked back at Mia. She sat down hard in the chair next to him and glared. He waited for her to start on him. Marc had had a lot of practice lately with hormonal women during pregnancy. He had three sisters-in-law. He was getting well versed on when to say something and when to run. He wished now he could run.

"I do not look 'fetching.' I look like a beached whale after four days in the sun. And if one more person says to me I look ready to 'pop,' I will pull my gun and 'pop' the fuck out of them." He barely refrained from laughing, but one of his team did not. "If you say one word, one single word to me Dennis, I will shoot you."

He nodded and sat very still. She looked back at Marc, and before he could tell her that he still had no replacement for her, the front doorbell sounded. She got up with a "don't move" and left them. Dennis asked if she was all right.

"She wants to go home and put her feet up and say to hell with this job, but she won't until we find someone to replace her. Anyone have someone they can recommend? She's going to kill us all if we don't."

Mia came back and said that one of his brothers was there to see him. He told everyone to find what they could on their victim and went to his office. He nearly left again when he saw Khan standing there.

"Have you found anything yet?" He shook his head and sat. "Damn it, Marc, you were supposed to find a vacation package for Mom and Dad over a week ago. What the hell is taking you so fucking long?"

"First you only asked me to look three days ago. And, second, I'm still under the opinion that sending them away on a cruise while you remodel the house is a bad idea. Mom likes her house just the way it is." Khan sat down and glared. "You can act like you're pissed at me all you want, but Monica agrees with me. Mom is going to be pissed when they come back and find that strangers have not only been in their home, but moved things around as well."

"What the hell am I supposed to do then? You tell me? Their house needs to be updated and modernized or it's going to fall down on them one of these days." Marc agreed with that and wished they'd just move in with Dylan and Jack as planned. But they were being stubborn and saying that newlyweds needed their alone time. They were both driving them all crazy.

"Why don't you talk to them about your plans like we've been saying to you for weeks? This is going to make them mad anyway that you're being highhanded." Marc left off the "again" in favor of keeping all his teeth. "Mom's still pissed at you for buying her and dad a new car."

"After we had to go pick her up twice at the store I had to do something. Besides, when she takes the kids somewhere, she needs a more reliable car. And for your information, they both like it now."

He knew they did. His mom just told him that morning that she was in love with the little SUV. Marc sat up in his chair and regarded his brother. He'd never seen him so relaxed before. Monica was good for him. Having a mate had the exact same effect on his older brothers. And he was happy for them. Jealous, too, if he was truthful about it.

Marc knew that he'd lost his chance at love a long time ago, as did his family. The female, Sonya Deed, a teenager he knew, had been his mate but had been killed in an automobile accident when she'd been seventeen and him only a year older. They didn't love one another and had only kissed, but it had been enough to break his heart and close it off even after all this time.

"Look, Khan, talk to her. She might surprise you. I'm willing to pay for the cruise myself if you just let them know what you want to do and ask them for her input. They might surprise you." Khan shifted in the seat and glared. "You can be grouchy with me all you want, but you know I'm right."

"Monica said the same thing. She said that when they came back and saw the house, they might move away and not live in the area again. She said that's what she would do if I was highhanded like that with her." Khan got up to pace. "You're right. Not that I'll tell anyone I said that, but you are. I'll talk to them tonight."

After he left, Marc picked up the phone and called his sister-in-law. "Well, Mon, it worked. He's going to talk to them tonight. Good job in giving him hell."

Her laughter made him smile. "He might live a bit longer if he would just listen to me on occasion. I tell you that man is as stubborn as Caitlynne is on a good day."

He agreed with her and told her he'd be over on Saturday if the case he was working on looked any better.

"It's an odd one. The woman was killed and someone tried to make it look like a big animal did it."

"Probably her husband. I'm sure you checked, but see if she had any insurance on her. I've been tempted to do the same with Khan lately." He told her that he had and there was nothing out of the ordinary there.

After they hung up, he went back to his meeting room and looked at the file. The husband was their first suspect, but he wasn't even in town when it happened, and the house had been ransacked too. Marc knew that the only way he was going to get his solved was if he went there and looked around himself.

"I'm going to go to the crime scene for a couple of weeks, maybe. Will you be all right until I get back? And I swear to you I'll hire the first person who looks like they can answer the phone when I get back." Mia glared at him when he told her. "I have been trying to find someone you like."

"I know you have." She stood up and stretched her back. "I'm so tired all I want to do is lie down on this desk and sleep until I go into labor. I'll keep looking while you're gone and if I find someone, you can interview them when you get back."

"If you find someone, hire them. I trust you. And you know what package and insurance whoever you hire will get, so go for it. Like I said, I trust you." She nodded. "And if she's single and pretty, make sure you tell them what a great boss I am and how much fun I am."

She snorted. "Like you'd even ask her out. You're like a hermit. It's work, home, and work again. How you going to meet Miss Right if that's the only places you go to see women?"

"I saw the woman I want and you got married to Jake. My loss is his gain, I suppose, but I think I see you more so it works out." He grinned when she slapped his arm playfully. "Besides, I don't have to get up in the middle of the night when the babies cry. I can just hear about it."

"You will meet someone someday, and I'm going to be the first to tell her what an ass you are. I'm sure after seeing you for ten minutes she'll know that too. But there you have it."

He went to his car and left the lot twenty minutes later. He knew that she saw the sadness, but he couldn't help it. There was just too much romance going on around his family right now and he couldn't take it. He loved them all, but he simply needed to get away.

CHAPTER 2

It had been three days of job hunting and Jonny was starving. She walked past dumpsters and thought about digging through them. She wasn't at that point yet, but she was very close. Walking back to the apartment, she watched a woman get out of her car with a large bag of food and thought about rolling her for it. Or maybe just scaring her enough so that she'd drop it and run. Then she turned around.

She was pregnant and huge with it. Jonny hadn't had a great deal of contact with pregnant women, but this woman looked wobbly and she wondered if she was going to make it inside. When she walked toward her building, Jonny thought she was going there, but she turned toward the one next to her at the last second. That's when the big truck flew past them.

Jonny was at her side, catching her, before she could think not to. Had she not gotten to her in time she would have fallen on her belly, and surely that couldn't have been good for the baby or the woman. She latched onto Jonny so hard that she was sure if she hadn't been a supernatural that she would have had a bruise. As it was now, she'd just have a small mark for an hour or so.

"He nearly…I was falling and…I need to sit down." She helped her into the building by using her keys, and then led her to sit in a chair. When she looked particularly pale, Jonny put her head down as far as it would go and not crunch her up with her belly.

Jonny left her sitting there and went to find a bathroom. She found one, as well as a nice kitchen, and wet some paper towels there and took them back to the woman with a glass of water. The woman took them gratefully and smiled when she'd taken a sip.

"I was concentrating so hard on what I had to do when I got back here that I didn't even see you or that truck. You saved me. I can't thank you enough."

Jonny nodded and realized that the scent of food was making her cat stir. She had to get out of there now or steal the woman's lunch. She stood to leave. Her belly took that moment to announce that it was empty.

"I have to go. I'm sure your husband will be able to help you back out to your car now if—"

"Please don't go. I'm the only one here and I'm still a little overwhelmed by what nearly happened." Jonny looked at the door thinking that she'd just watch her from the other side until someone came. "I'll feed you."

"I don't need your charity." The bark of her words embarrassed her. "I have to go, miss. I'm sure you're going to be just fine now."

"You sit down right now." There was a command there that she couldn't ignore. The woman was human but she sounded like she was used to getting her way, so Jonny sat down.

When she nearly tumbled out of the chair, Jonny stood up and helped her. The woman really was a bit unsteady on her feet as Jonny helped her back to the tiny little kitchen.

“I’m going to sit in the kitchen with you while you eat this meal. I’m so upset right now that if I tried I’d be sick, and throwing up is not very comfortable in any state, but this big, I can’t hardly sit on the commode, much less puke in one.” She started for the door and stopped to hold onto the desk. “Lock the door again, will you? I have to sit down again.”

Jonny did as she asked and helped her to the kitchen. She wanted the food more than anything, but she wasn’t going to eat it. She had to find something soon or she would be stealing money to purchase it. She owed the man with the shop more than she’d wanted to right now.

“I’m Mia Bowmen. In case you didn’t notice, I’m going to have a baby in a couple of months. Twins actually. Do sit down.” Jonny sat, and the bag of food was shoved in front of her. “If you don’t eat this I’m going to throw it out. You will be missing a great meal too. Roast beef sandwich with Swiss cheese and a dill pickle. There’s also potato salad and some cheesecake in there.”

Jonny’s stomach rumbled louder. She reached for the sandwich that the woman had unwrapped as she spoke and took the first bite. It was like heaven in her mouth. She was halfway through the twelve-inch sub before she realized that she was being handed a fork and the salad. She nearly moaned at the taste of her favorite way to have potatoes. She was eating the cake when Mia spoke.

“When was the last time you ate?” Jonny flushed and looked at the crumbs on the table, all that was left of her lunch. “You just ate an entire meal in less than ten minutes, so don’t shy away from me now. When?”

“Five days ago. I left where I was. Then I’ve been looking for work since. I don’t have any identification, so I can't get a job." She nodded at her. "I'll pay you back for this. I'm sorry that I made a pig of myself, but...."

"You were hungry. Don't worry about it. And I'll be honest with you now because you were with me, it was my husband's dinner, not my lunch. I ate mine at the deli. But he won't even miss what he didn't know he was getting." She stood up and got three bottles of water out of the refrigerator. "I'm looking for someone to take my place so I can go on maternity leave. Can you type and answer the phone?"

"Yes. But I don't...." Jonny looked at the table again instead of the nice woman. "I can't work for you. I have to find a job that I can get paid in cash. I can't...I can't be found."

"You let me worry about that part. I'm in charge of this little office. Marc may think he is but I run the place. What's your name, or is that going to be a problem too?" Jonny nodded. "Okay, I have to call you something. How about...Joan? Joan Savior?"

"Why?" Jonny looked confused. "Why are you helping me? For all you know I could be some kind of mass murderer and want to work here to hide until the next job is complete."

"You could be, I suppose, but I doubt a mass murderer would have helped a rotund woman who nearly got knocked on her ass by a semi. And you were honest with me. You didn't have to be. You could have let me fall, then kicked me when you passed me."

"No I couldn't have." Mia smiled, and Jonny flushed again. "You're going to hire me and pay me under the table because you nearly fell and feel grateful. In the morning, you might feel differently."

"I doubt it. Come on, Joan, let's get you trained." They walked back out to the desk after cleaning up. "You now work for Bowen Investigations. The owner is Marc Bowen, and he's about the best boss in the world. And he's cute. I'm not sure if anyone would call him handsome, but I am married to the most handsome man in the world."

After giving her a note pad and a pen, Mia went through the entire office. She didn't once wobble and Jonny had a feeling she'd been had. She wanted to ask her about it but she didn't want to make her mad. She had a job and it was going to keep her off the grid so that Roy wouldn't find her.

At five o'clock Mia was telling her how to turn the phones over to the service. "You'll need a cell phone and I'll have it for you tomorrow. Sometimes when it's an emergency the service will call me and I can call Marc. He trusts my judgment on when to call him. I do if I can't decide if he needs to be called or not. Sometimes it's nothing, but there are enough times that it's something. He's okay with the occasional blunder."

After locking down the office, Jonny turned to her. "My name is Jonny Thomas. I'm being chased and I can't go back there."

"Thank you. You don't know how much it means to me that you trust me with this. I won't tell anyone and we'll keep calling you Joan. Your paperwork will be just enough that you can get paid, and from there we'll work something else out." She handed her some money and Jonny backed away. "You have to eat. I've taken it out of petty cash and you can pay it back when you get your first check. I assume you have somewhere to stay that's safe?"

She nodded. "I'm living in an empty building. I'll…as soon as I can I'll find somewhere else, but for now this is all I can do."

"You'll be safe, that's all I care about right now." She locked the door and turned to her. "I'll be in at eight-thirty tomorrow morning. The rest of them will be in around nine or so. Marc won't be back for a couple more weeks unless he can figure this case out. I'll see you tomorrow then?"

"Yes, I'll be here. And thank you for everything." Jonny watched her walk to her car and she moved up the street. She walked past her building and to the next block before she went down an alley and returned. She never left or came back to her building the same way twice. Careful of the streets and watching for Roy, she entered her building and went up the stairs before she took out the money.

Five hundred dollars. She'd given her a fortune. Jonny was dancing around the room when she realized that she could go and get some food for herself. Not to mention some of the basic needs of her living there. She needed soap and shampoo. The cleaning solution she'd been using was hot to her skin and her body was drying out from it. Her hair, too, needed something more than the dish detergent she'd found. She counted out the money again, and leaving all but two hundred dollars of it, left to find a store.

It took her nearly an hour to find a Wal-Mart. She spent ten minutes trying to find the right shampoo, having so much fun that she nearly left after getting it just to go and wash her hair. Then she got the rest of the things on her list, including a large backpack to carry things in. She got her a plate and silverware, along with a single pan. She wasn't much on cooking but might want a cup of tea sometime, and she could heat up soup too. When she left she'd filled the pack and had three bags as well.

Putting things away was also fun. She was careful when purchasing things to make sure she could leave them without problems if she were found. The place didn't have electricity, but it did have hot water and a gas stove. Keeping things cold was a problem, but she hadn't bought anything that needed to stay cold, so she thought she'd be all right. By nine she was putting her twenty-two dollars in her stash and went to bed.

~~~

Reed watched the girl while she worked. He knew that she was a panther and figured she knew he was one as well. She never said anything to him about it, and he, too, let it go. For now. Reed knew that no one in Marc's office knew he was a cat and figured that was fine. When Mia had called him last night to ask him to come by and set up access for her new employee, as well as a cell phone, he'd been happy. He wasn't sure what to think now.

"She'll need to have it programmed like mine is with all the numbers. Can you do that for her?" Reed nodded at Mia. "She's going to do just fine, I think. By this time next week I can be at home and getting ready for the twins."

"You think she'll be able to handle this on her own? She doesn't look all that sure of herself." He knew he was making her nervous but didn't know why. "She looks terrified out of her mind."

"She'll be just fine. And don't you go scaring her off either. I need this, Reed, and she's going to make it happen." He nodded at her and smiled. "I like her. A great deal, and she saved me yesterday from falling. She didn't have to do that."
~~~

She'd told him how she'd come to meet Joan twice now. He didn't want to sound suspicious but it just sounded too…well, it sounded like she'd been at the right place at the right time too easily. He decided to have Caitlynne run a check on her.

"I don't know what's going on in your mind right now, but I swear to you if you run a check on this girl I will make you pay." He looked at Mia, shocked. First, because he swore she'd read his mind, and second that she'd threatened him.

"I have to know that my family will be safe, Mia. She's working for one of my brothers. What if she tries to hurt one of them? You know that they're always coming in and out of here."

"Please don't. I'm begging you not to look up anything." She looked around before continuing. "I think she has a husband or boyfriend looking for her and she's terrified he'll find her. You wouldn't believe what she looked like yesterday when I offered her this job. She was terrified when she told me she'd have to find work that paid in cash."

"She didn't ask you for the job?" She shook her head. "Well, that doesn't mean she didn't plan that either. But if after this week she doesn't do anything stupid, I won't have Caitlynne look, deal?"

She nodded. He just hoped that he hadn't made a huge mistake. He finished the phone and set up the computer. He was sitting close to her, showing her how to change her password to something she'd know when he realized two things.

Joan had never been near another panther, male or otherwise, besides him, and she was much smarter than she'd let them believe. She knew how to run a computer as well as he did. Whoever was chasing her wasn't a boyfriend or husband, but someone else. He could also smell her fear.

"Have you registered?" She looked up at him when he'd whispered to her. "With the local male, have you registered?"

"Registered? I don't understand? I have to register with someone to work here? Mia said so long as I never went on cases that I'd be fine in the office."

He realized something else about her right then. She had no clue. Neither of what he was nor that she was supposed to follow rules set up by other panthers. He stepped back from her, wondering how to make her understand. She was still looking at him.

"You're going to be fine. I thought…I guess I thought you'd go out on assignments like Mia did before she got pregnant." He was babbling and shut up. He showed her how to access the phone and asked her if she had any questions. She shook her head. He might have promised he'd not talk to Caitlynne about her, but he needed to talk to Khan. He called him when he left the offices.

"I need to talk to you. You know about when I can come in?" He told him now would be good and asked him what it was about. "I think it would be better in person. Besides, I need to think about this. Okay?"

He was walking into the Towers a few minutes later and in Khan's office just after that. He sat down, then jumped and started to pace. He hadn't touched Joan but knew that Khan could smell her on him. Reed sat again and looked at him.

"I was just at Marc's office. Mia had me set up a cell and computer access for her new employee. Her name is Joan Savior, she's a panther." Khan leaned back and nodded as Reed continued. "I think that there is something going on. At first I thought it was a set up but now—"

"Now what? You…is she your mate?" Reed shook his head and Khan continued. "Okay then, what's the problem? She didn't hurt Mia, did she?"

"No, nothing like that. She's…." Reed got up to pace again. "Mia seems to think she's running from a boyfriend or husband. Joan told her that she couldn't work for her when she offered her the job because she couldn't take a job where she'd be found. I don't think Joan is her real name either. And I promised Mia that I'd not look into her either via Caitlynne."

"So you came to me so I could ask her to look into it for you? I don't think so. When you make a promise like that it's implied that you won't go around the bush to get what you want. Not from Mia or anyone."

"No. Nothing like that. I don't…what if I told you that I don't think she knew what I was? What if I said that I got the feeling from her that she's…terrified of what she is, for more reasons than someone chasing her? She seemed to be…I know this sounds really stupid, but I get the feeling that she thinks she's the only one of her kind."

"You think that's why she's being chased, because she's a cat?" Reed nodded and sat back down. "Why? I mean you'd not be able to smell that on her. What makes you think that?"

He looked at his brother hard and decided that he was right. "She didn't know what I was talking about when I asked her if she had registered with you. She didn't know. And she wasn't lying either. She simply doesn't know."

"You want me to go and talk to her?" Reed nodded and frowned when Khan shook his head. "Nah, we'll leave it to Marc to deal with. He owes me for siding with Monica about Mom and Dad on the cruise. You and I will look around and I might just go by there to see Mia tomorrow and check her out. If I see what you see, we'll wait. If she's faking it, we'll call in Dylan. He can find out sooner than most of us anyway."

Reed liked that plan. But he thought maybe he'd keep an eye on her as well. Marc was gone and he felt it his responsibility to watch over his business while he was away. Besides, she was a beauty, and maybe he'd ask her out if this turned out to be nothing more than a woman running from someone.

CHAPTER 3

Marc walked the crime scene again. There were so many imprints there that he was having a hard time figuring out who was who. He thought maybe there had been at least three dozen people in this room as recently as a week ago. He knelt down to the stained floor again.

He could smell her blood and knew that she'd been terrified when she'd been laying there dying. He looked at the size of the stain and thought maybe she'd bled quickly and had died within minutes. But that didn't ring true with the cuts on her. Marc looked up when he heard someone enter the room. It was the chief of police in this town.

"You said that she didn't have any other marks on her but the ones that marred her, right?" Eric Campos nodded. "Yet there doesn't seem to be nearly enough blood for her to have bled to death, do you think?"

"I thought the same thing. Even had one of the coroner guys run tests to see if she was indeed all emptied out like they said. She was." He bounced on his heels for a few seconds. "Could it be a blood sucker?"

Marc shook his head. He and Eric had been friends for nearly all their lives, and he knew as much about Marc as Marc did about him. Eric was simply a human, but he was a telepath as well.

"Then I'm at a loss. I was thinking of that murder we had a few years ago, the one you came and helped me on. Remember it?" Marc nodded and stood up. "She was beat up pretty bad, and we nearly didn't see the marks on her throat until we'd been about to send her to her family. You saw them when none of us could."

"But I smelled him on her first. I don't smell anything like that here." Eric nodded. "What do you think happened here?"

"Her husband hired someone to kill her and make it look like some animal did it. But he panicked for some reason and killed her here and had to get rid of the blood." Eric knelt down to the stain as he handed Marc a picture. "See that? The heel print? It was here when I got here, but after a while of her laying here and bleeding and waiting on the asses at the morgue to show up, it covered it."

It was there, a little of the heel. He looked at it, then at the stain, and moved to where the heel would have been. Taking out his pocketknife, he asked if he could cut below the carpet, and was told that they were done with this room as far as evidence went.

Marc cut deep through the carpet and lifted a large square of it up. There on the padding was a perfect outline of the boot, also all the extra blood they'd missed. The padding was soaked with it. Eric grinned up at him.

"Wouldn't have thought of that. I guess when he was standing here she'd already bled enough through the carpet to leave the print." Marc nodded and lifted it to his nose. "Whatcha got?"

"Male, human pissed." He looked at the closet, then back at Eric. "Maybe we should check the closet now. We have probable cause."

Eric had told him that the only place they could look was the floor. The homeowner and the husband of the dead woman had said that anything else was off limits. Eric pulled out his cell and made a call.

"Hey, Judy, can I talk at your husband? Tell him it's important." After talking for several minutes to the judge in the town, he and Eric waited on the judge to sign off on a search warrant and have it brought to them. They both knew that the room was being watched, and looked up at the newly installed camera and smiled.

"You figure a pair of his boots is gonna have blood on them?" Marc nodded. "You really sure or are you guessing you're sure?"

"I'll smell them before you bag them, but I'm sure that he wouldn't have gotten rid of them." He sat down on the chair and looked at Eric when he sat in the other one. "When the maid came into the house the night she was found, you said that he was in the kitchen and that he'd sent the maid up to find his wife. She said that she'd commented on his boots and that they were muddy." Eric nodded.

"If that is the same pair, he wouldn't have been able to get rid of them then or since because we've been watching the house. Anything going out would have been searched, and he's even being watched at work. We're telling him that it's as a precaution, but I think he knows that we suspect him. He's a bit cagey."

They got the warrant twenty minutes later and Eric went to the closet with one of his officers in tow. He lifted one of the three pairs of boots from the rack and handed them to his officer, nearly dropping them on Marc, who'd been kneeling close by. It was a trick they had perfected over the years to get Marc a good whiff of whatever was being handled. Marc shook his head.

The second pair of boots was it. Marc stood up and backed away, signaling to Eric he'd hit pay dirt. They bagged up the third pair because they had to, and Eric had the officer take them to the lab. As soon as he was gone the door to the bedroom opened and three men came in.

It was the man himself, Jeff Ansell the widower, and his attorneys more than likely. "You have no right to look anywhere but the bloodstains. Anything you find in this house is—"

Eric slapped the warrant against the first attorney's chest and smiled. "That says I can look anywhere I want, and I did. As soon as the tests come back positive, I'm going to enjoy arresting you."

Jeff lashed out at Eric. Eric had him on the floor in seconds. The man was screaming about wild animals and such by the time he was being cuffed. When Eric lifted him off the floor, Jeff looked wild, insane, and pissed.

"I'll sue you for this. I'll own everything you have by the end of the day." Eric nodded as he escorted him from the room and told him his rights. "I'll even own your cat if you have one, and all your pension."

"I don't have a cat because my friend there says that they'd be pissy every time he came over. Even if it was a male and a female wouldn't be much better. I don't have a pension thanks to my ex-wife's blood-sucking lawyer, and he is that, by the way. I do have a nice television, but it's not working so well right now. The football team I was watching the other night made a stupid play and I sort of threw my shoe through it. But it's yours if you want it. Might get you a nice boyfriend while you're in prison if you got it fixed up and hung it in your cell."

Marc spent another night in town after hanging out at the bar until all hours of the night with Eric. The tests had come back positive for blood, and Ansell was being put into an orange suit and taken to the cells by the time Marc had his first drink. Now he was loading his suitcase into the trunk of his car and getting ready to leave.

"You should just move down here. We could get into trouble every weekend instead of once in a while." Eric had on sunglasses even though it was cloudy. Marc felt the same way, like his eyeballs had been run through salt and put back in his head backwards.

"If I lived here I'd be dead within a month and you know it." He grinned at Eric. "I'm too old for this shit. Next time let's just go and get some pancakes with whipped cream and call it a night."

Eric laughed hard, then snapped his mouth closed and grabbed his head. "Fucking bastard, you did that on purpose."

Marc laughed as well and hugged his friend goodbye. "I have to get going. I have a very pregnant secretary back home that I have to find a replacement for before her and her husband murder me. I wouldn't mind it so much right now, but I might in a day or two when my head doesn't hurt so much."

It took Marc nearly ten hours to drive home, and by the time he showered and got into bed, it was well after four that afternoon. Knowing that no one was expecting him until Monday and it was only Saturday, he decided to sleep until he woke before he called anyone to let them know he was home.

The pounding at the door made him snarl. He looked at the clock by his bed and had to look again. It had been nearly sixteen hours since he'd gotten to bed. He staggered down the stairs but nearly went back up them when he saw Khan standing on the porch.

"You'll let me in or so help me I'll break this fucking door down." Marc opened the door and stepped back. "You get back into town after being gone for over two weeks and don't say a word to anyone? You prick, you have any idea how worried I was when I called Eric and asked him where you were and he said you'd left hours ago?"

"I was exhausted and didn't think anyone would mind if I slept it off. Want some tea?" He went to the kitchen, knowing that Khan would either follow or go home. He hoped he'd go home but that was just too much to hope for.

"Did you solve the murder?" Marc nodded as he pulled down the tealeaves from his cabinet. "I suppose that's good. Who did it? Her husband?"

"Yes. He was having an affair with his secretary and his wife found out. She told him she was kicking him out, as she had all the money, and he took exception to that. If they would have divorced, he wouldn't have collected anything. Murder like this one would have given him everything times two. So tell Monica she was right."

"No thanks. She's hard enough to live with right now. She's mad at me because I haven't talked to Mom yet." Marc rolled his eyes. "Speaking of secretary, Mia hired you one while you were gone. She's a cat."

Marc nearly dropped his tea maker and turned to look at Khan. "What do you mean she hired a cat? Mia doesn't know what we are, nor does the rest of my team. Please tell me you didn't tell them?"

"No, I didn't, though I think you should. They seem like a great bunch." Marc sat down, holding onto his pot. "I went to see Joan."

"And?" Marc got up to finish the tea and then looked into his refrigerator, knowing that he was avoiding his brother. He didn't come here to tell him about Monica or the new secretary. There was more.

"She doesn't seem to recognize that we're the same. Reed noticed it first when he went to set her up with a phone. When I went to see her on the pretense that I needed to see Dewey about something, she didn't react at all. I thought she was either a good actress or like Reed said." Khan stretched out his legs as he continued. "I sent Monica over a couple of days later to meet her. She really is clueless."

Marc didn't want to hear the rest, but he knew that Khan was upset about something that Monica had found when she'd read the other woman's mind. He finished with the tea and sat with his brother while it brewed.

"Just fucking tell me. Is she there to kill me, one of the other family members now? And so you know, if it's you, I might help her." Khan shook his head and smiled. "Tell me, Khan."

"She's being chased by a man named Roy Dawson. Monica said that she has a block on her mind that's pretty tight, so I had Reed look this prick up. He deals in exotic animals. You think he wants to sell her to one of those people he deals with?"

"Why would he do that knowing that she's going to shift at some point, and then where will he be?" The timer sounded and he got up to pour them both a cup. "Did you ask her what was going on?"

"No. I was leaving that up to you to find out. You're the investigator. Also, something else. Joan isn't her name and Monica refused to look into Mia's mind to find out if she knew. We're pretty sure she does, because she's really protective of the girl. Also...."

Marc sat the two cups on the table and thought that if he could, he'd find someone to murder his brother. All these bits and pieces of information about his place of business were driving him nuts. Marc slammed the cookie tin in from of Khan and snarled at him to fucking tell him it all.

"She's a virgin." Marc looked at his brother, wondering why the hell he thought that information was needed. "She has to be protected by us now. We can't let anything happen to her until she finds her mate." He waited for Khan to laugh or to say he was kidding, but he just stared at him. For whatever reason, that pissed him off more. Of all the old-fashioned idiotic things to say, this had to be the topper.

"Are you fucking kidding me? What do you propose we do, Khan? Find a chastity belt and strap it on her? Maybe we can follow her around from now on, and when another male comes near her we can slash his throat and hope she doesn't notice all the blood."

"That's not what I meant, you jack ass. I meant that we can't let this Dawson person find her in the event that he wants her for himself. What if he rapes her thinking that he can get her pregnant or something?"

Marc took his tea from him and dumped it in the sink. Then he took the cookie Khan had in his hand and put it in the trash before going to the door. He opened it and took several deep breaths before he spoke to Khan.

"Get out. I mean it, Khan, get out." Khan started to speak but he cut him off. "I don't care if she's a virgin, but I'm reasonably sure that she's been one longer than you ever were. And she stayed that way because she could fight men off or she simply doesn't care for sex. Either way, she's a virgin by choice and I for one could care less. If she needs my help with this person, I'll help her, but I'm not going to stalk a woman because you're a Neanderthal who has yet to come to this century."

"I'm just saying that now that she works for you that you're going to need to keep on top of things concerning her. She doesn't strike me as the asking for help type." Marc nodded as Khan went out the door. "She's very beautiful, even Monica says so."

"I don't care how beautiful she is, Khan. I have had my mate and she's gone. Falling in love with her is not going to happen, if that's what you're thinking." Khan flushed with embarrassment. "I'm glad you're thinking of me like that, but I'm not going to find love like you and the others have. And I'm fine with it."

"I love you, Marc. I only want to see you happy. And this girl…I thought she'd make you smile again and not work all the time."

After Khan left he went back up to his bedroom, then to the bathroom to shower. He was standing under the spray when he thought of what Khan had said. Marc thought it was time he left the area. Maybe go down and stay with Eric for a while, until he knew want he wanted to do. Maybe he'd see the world like he'd planned to do after college. Anything but stay there and have his family try and set him up. It hurt too much.

By lunch he had most of his laundry finished and his shirts ready to go to the cleaners. Pulling up his calendar, he saw that first thing Monday he had an appointment with someone from the sheriff's office, and then he had another appointment with the same man at one. Great, she was already fucking up his day. Making a note for her to let him know which time was the correct one, he called his office and retrieved messages. After that he sat down to file a report on the murder, and then he went into town to have some dinner. It was only nine when he went to bed. Setting his alarm, he laid down, trying to word how he was going to tell his family that he was selling his house and leaving within the month. They were going to be pissed no matter what he said, and was preparing for that as well.

His phone chirped once, then went silent at around four in the morning. As he didn't recognize the number, he didn't answer it and let it go to voicemail. When that notification sounded, he was nearly asleep and thought he'd get it in a minute when all of a sudden his alarm was going off. It was morning. He was in the shower when he remembered to check the message, and forgot when he went downstairs to find that his refrigerator was broken. He was over an hour late getting to work because he had to find a repair man as well as deal with all the food getting warm.

CHAPTER 4

Jonny tried the number again and it went straight to voicemail. She was getting frustrated as she set her lunch on the counter at work and put her bottle of water in the refrigerator. She smiled at Sheri Pitts, one of the other people in the offices, as she came in looking like she'd spent the better part of the morning doing her makeup. The woman always looked like she was ready to go down a ramp like a fashion model. She was also extremely nice.

"You have anything for a headache?" Jonny shook her head. "I bet you never have headaches, do you? You look so healthy that a headache or any other form of sickness would shy away from you."

Jonny didn't answer, because Sheri was right. She never got sick and she rarely got a headache. She supposed it was because she was a freak. As Shari put her coffee in a mug, Jonny went back to her little desk. She saw that the door to the office was open again and shut it as she sat down and took the phones off service. She was answering the man at the other end when a gorgeous man walked in, stepped by her, and entered the office behind her. She supposed he didn't see her with the phone that he was screaming into plastered to his head, but she went in right behind him and waited for him to stop so she could find out what he was doing there. When he put his phone down and buried his head in his hands, she cleared her throat.

"Unless you have a very horrible cold and are clearing your throat to tell me something, I would suggest you get out of here. I've had a shitty morning so far and I'm in no mood to screw with anyone right now."

"Well that's good for you, but I don't have a cold and you don't have an appointment. I would know because I would have made it for you. As for you being in this office, you know that you're not supposed to be here either. You're name isn't on the desk placard and not on the door. Well, no one's is on the door, but I know it wouldn't be yours."

He lifted his head, and she nearly took a step back. Christ, he was more than gorgeous. He was…eatable. She cleared her throat again and he cocked a brow at her. She didn't squirm like she wanted to, but lifted her chin a little higher when he looked like he was going to laugh at her.

"Now see here. You need to get out of this office right now before Mr. Bowen comes in. He has…he has a nasty temper, and once he lets it go, you'll…you'll regret it." He leaned back in the chair and she had a thought. She took a step back, then another before he finally spoke.

"Don't move." She stopped, not really sure why she'd obeyed him but she had and now she was stuck there. "I'm assuming that you're my new secretary."

She nodded and turned her head to see the distance between her and the door. She could make it, she figured, and turned her body to leave when he suddenly grabbed her arm. Without thought as to what she was doing, she slammed her free hand into his nose, then kicked him in the groin. Jonny took off to the door again and tripped when he grabbed her ankle.

"Stop right fucking now before I hurt one of us." She kicked out at his face and nearly connected when he yanked her hard toward him. Before she could move he was laying over her and holding her hands above her head. She tried to bite him but he was too quick. She froze when a voice from the doorway spoke.

"You two have met, I see. Marc, this is Joan Savior. Joan, this is our boss, Marc Bowen. Marc is usually a really nice guy once you get to know him, but occasionally he needs the shit knocked out of him like you did. Are you bleeding?"

She looked up at the man who still held her down and noticed the blood on his nose and lip. Jonny had the most incredible urge to lick him. Shuddering, she shoved him off her, and she was pretty sure he let her. They stood up together, and he told Dennis Gibbs, the other man in the offices, to watch the phones while he talked to her.

She stood when the door closed and continued to do so after he told her to sit. It was on the tip of her tongue to ask him if he wanted her to pee on a sheet of paper too, but bit her lip instead.

"I'm not mad. Hurt but not mad at you. So why don't you have a seat?" He sat behind his desk again and wiped at his mouth with a tissue. "We can start over from here if you want."

"Am I fired?" She liked working there and she loved the money she made. She'd managed to save over seven hundred dollars and had been putting it in plastic bags in her backpack she carried with her everywhere now.

"No. I made a mistake by not introducing myself to you. Then I grabbed you. You were reacting like a woman who didn't know her attacker. Now that we know each other, I hope you won't have cause to hit me again." She mumbled that she wasn't sure about that, and he laughed. She hadn't thought she'd said it that loud.

"I'm Marc Bowen, owner of this establishment. I heard from my family that you're replacing Mia while she's out on medical leave." She nodded and glanced at the door when the phone rang. "He's done it before, so he knows what he's doing."

"Did you mess with the calendar?" He tried to think what she meant with her subject change so quickly, and nodded.

"You had the same appointment set up for different times of the day." She started shaking her head. "Yes, you did. One for nine-thirty, the other for one this afternoon."

"He needed both appointments. One before his court appearance this morning, then the second one to ask you about some work after the hearing. He said depending on how it went he wanted to ask you for help. The service filled the slot again and now he's out in the cold. And when I tried to call you, you didn't answer."

The phone call he'd not recognized. So far he was batting at a negative with her. He started to stand when she stiffened. She might put on a brave front, but she was afraid of him. He sat back down.

"I screwed up and I'm sorry. When Danny comes in I'll tell him what I did and meet him for lunch. Does that fix it?" She shrugged. "Are you going to have a seat? If my mom comes in here and you're standing while I'm sitting she'll box my ears."

She mumbled again and waited for him to say something. She was pretty sure he'd heard her again, but since he didn't comment on her thinking he'd been hatched and not born, she sat down. She'd have to stop saying things under her breath if she was going to work with this man. He must have the hearing of a bat. When he nodded at her, she tried not to fidget, another bad habit she had when she was nervous.

"Tell me about yourself." She looked at him, trying to figure out his angle. He had to have one. Men didn't want to know about the people who worked for them, especially men like the one in front of her. Not to mention she was pretty sure he knew everything about her. Well, nearly everything. She wondered what he'd do if she suddenly became a great big black panther in front of him.

"I don't know what you want to know. Mia Bowmen hired me and she said that I'd be fine here." She'd actually told her that she'd be safe here, but she didn't trust that any more than she did Roy. "If you're not going to fire me, I have work to do."

"I'm not going to fire you. I just…I would like to get to know you, that's all. I like knowing all the people who work for me."

She stood up and so did he. She waited for him to do something, move toward her, attack, but he simply stayed where he was. Jonny moved to the door slowly, backing to it so she could keep an eye on him.

"I won't hurt you. You can trust me on that." She nodded but didn't answer him. "You don't believe me, do you?"

"I don't know you well enough to believe anything you say to me. And I don't trust anyone. Everyone lies to get what they want. The trick is finding out early on what it is so you can figure out if you want to give it to them or not. It's the best way of dealing with people."

"I don't want anything from you but a good day's work." She nodded again. "I guess you don't trust me on that either."

"I'll give you a good day's work, Mr. Bowen, but that's all. I want to work here, but it's not the end of the world if I don't. I'll just move on." She touched the doorjamb with her fingertips and reached for the door. "If you grab me again, I will kill you."

She shut the door behind her as she left his office. Sitting in her chair, she had to put her head between her knees and breathe several times before she felt she could stand again. There was something about him, something that wasn't really terrifying but scary. She staggered to the kitchen to get herself something to drink. She was sitting at her desk again when Marc's first appointment showed up.

~~~

"Are you even listening to me?" Marc looked at his mom and tried to think what they'd been talking about when she answered his question. "I see. And what case are you trying to solve while you're having dinner with me? If I wanted to have a meal with someone who didn't listen to me I'd eat with your dad. I do hope it's a nice divorce case and you're only required to take pictures instead of getting the snot beat out of you again."

"No divorce is nice, Mom, and you know that. Think of all the humans you know that have gotten them. Have any of them said, 'Well that was special. Let's marry again so we can go through that again'? I doubt it. No, I was thinking about the girl who works for me. Something about her bothers me."

"Like what? I talked to her the other day. She's very…I was going to say stubborn, but that's not it. She's very distrusting, isn't she? I get the feeling that whatever is in that pretty little head of hers is frightening." The waiter sat their dinners in front of them and he had a sudden thought as to what Joan might be eating tonight.
~~~

"I don't suppose she told you where she lives, did she? I've tried finding it out from Mia, and she told me to behave and to leave her alone before she quits me. Why would she quit? I'm an easy person to work for." She'd been working for him for two weeks since he'd been back, and all she'd said to him was who was there and that she was going to lunch. He hated that she wouldn't speak to him about anything.

"Perhaps she doesn't like you very much and doesn't want you to know. Ever think about that?" She laughed when he snorted at her. "She is very quiet. Monica says she had a good lock on her mind, but she said she's not going to try and breach it. I personally think she knows more about Joan than she's saying, but that's neither here nor there."

So did he. He wished that Jack and Dylan would get back so he could have him look into her mind and find out. But they were at their cabin for the summer months and he didn't want to disturb them. They loved it there, and when they came back, they were so refreshed and happy that he hated to ask them to do this for him. But she was driving him crazy.

"I think she might be homeless." That made him look at his mother, and he asked her why she said that. "Did you ever notice that Mia comes by on payday twice? I think she's helping her cash her checks. And when she returns, Joan looks so relieved that she can hardly breathe through it. I don't think she trusts that Mia will return with her money."

He had no idea and he was supposed to be this great detective. He decided that the next time checks went out he'd pay more attention. He realized then that he had no idea when payday actually was. Damn it, he was a slug, and was going to start paying attention to the everyday things in his office.

He ate his meal, trying to think of why this woman, of all the women he knew, was on his mind so much. He looked up at his mom when she laughed. He flushed, knowing that he'd missed something again.

"She's got you all twisted up, doesn't she? I wonder why." He said that he wished he knew as well. "Have you slept with her yet?"

He nearly choked to death on his drink. When she smiled at him, he decided that she'd been teasing him. He started to tell her it wasn't the least bit funny when she spoke again.

"Marc, why do you hold yourself back from women?" He wasn't sure how to answer that, so he didn't. "You're a good man. You have a great job, money in the bank, and you're not too bad to look at either. That is when you clean up and don't wear those horrible ties. Why don't you ask her out? Ask her back to your place for a roll in the hay or whatever you men call it these days."

"I'm not discussing my sex life or the lack of one with you. I'll have you know that she's not really my type. I'm more of the…." Christ, he hadn't been out in so long he had no idea what this type was. "I go for the more flashy type of women. The kind that doesn't cringe whenever I'm near them and doesn't avoid getting closer than a foot to me every time I'm speaking to her."

He realized he'd said too much when she looked at him oddly. He started to change the subject but he found he couldn't. Really, he wasn't sure if he wanted to talk to his mom about Joan, but he had to speak to someone.

"The first day I came back from Illinois I was on the phone getting a repair man to come out and see if he could fix my fridge. I walked past her without seeing her. She came into my office and nearly threw me out. I touched her." He sat back in his chair, no longer hungry. "I grabbed her arm to stop her from leaving and she hit me and then…unmanned me. When I grabbed her foot to stop her again, she broke my nose with her foot. I had to hold her down to keep her from hurting me. After I apologized to her and told her she wasn't being fired, she looked at me and told me if I touched her again, grabbed her, she'd kill me. I believe her."

"You frightened her." He nodded at his mom. "And since, what have you done to make it up to her?"

"I'm at my wits' end with trying to get her to trust me. I'm not upset about her saying that to me. Hell, I feel like I'm lucky that she didn't kill me. But…." Marc looked at the people in the restaurant as he continued. "She brings the same thing every day to lunch. Those dried noodles in a bag that she cooks in the microwave, and bottled water. I checked on how much they cost, and you know you can get like a dozen of them for less than five bucks. She never goes out to lunch with anyone, and she wears the same five shirts every week. She has no coat to speak of, and her shoes are worn through."

"You want to help her." He nodded, still watching the room and not his mom. He didn't want her to see how affected he was by this. But he was pretty sure she'd figured it out.

"I don't want to just help her, Mom, I need to. I find myself thinking of her instead of work more hours of the day than I should. When she comes into my office I find that I can't seem to breathe until she leaves again, and then her scent is all over the office for hours after she leaves." He looked at her then. "And she hates me."

She looked at him for a long minute, then another before she spoke to him. Marc took her hand when she reached for it, suddenly afraid she was going to tell him something he didn't want to know about Joan.

"Marc, have you given any thought as to why you feel this way about her? I mean, beyond her working for you. Do you know what it sounds like when you talk about her?"

He let go of her hand and stood. The waitress brought him the check and he took it before his mom could. He wasn't going to dignify what his mom was implying with an answer. As he started to walk away, she spoke again.

"It happens, Marc. Cats that lose their mates for one reason or another find another later in life. It might be just as you, too, believe it to be…she's your other half. Sonya was so young and so were you, maybe this is your second—"

"I had a chance, Mom. And she died. There will never be anyone to replace her and you know it." He stretched his neck and body, calming his cat before he continued. "Please don't bring this up again. I won't…I can't think along those lines only to be hurt again when it turns out not to be her, and she leaves me again. I can't do that again."

She stood up and hugged him, and he felt tears in his eyes. He'd not cried since he'd been told that Sonya had been killed, and wasn't going to give into them now. After helping his mom on with her coat, he walked her to her car.

"Marc, I love you son. And I'm sorry that I upset you. Will you forgive me?" He told her not to be ridiculous and kissed her cheek.

He helped her into her car and drove home. It wasn't late, but he needed a good run. Stripping down, he shifted and ran for over three hours until he was nearly falling over with exhaustion before he even went into his house. But as soon as his head hit the pillow, he was wide awake and wondering if Joan was warm enough or if she had enough food to eat.

"This is stupid. Tomorrow morning I'm going to kiss her and then that will be the end of this. Once I stop thinking about how she will taste, I can move on with my life and get some work done." As he rolled over, he knew that he could no more go in and kiss her as he could stop working. He was going to have to do something and soon.

CHAPTER 5

"Have you found her yet?" Roy wasn't sure why he was asking. He was pretty sure that they'd let him know if they had. But it had been almost a whole month and he had orders to fill so he could get inside the house. He looked at the ledger in front of him when Harris answered.

"Been no sign of her since she left here near about three weeks ago. I'm thinking she either left town with a stranger or she's holed up somewhere with a friend." Roy knew that wouldn't happen. Jonny didn't have any friends except for Anita.

"I have a request for nine panthers, and no panthers. I have fucking wolves out my ass and a bear but not one fucking panther." He looked down at the numbers that had been coming in since she left. "I could make twice that with the amount of money the rich and stupid would pay for her. And she won't play the game."

Harris shook his head. "She's a stubborn one, she is. When I think of all that money you offered her and she threw it back in your face? Makes me want to find her and beat her something good."

An empty threat and they both knew it. She'd kill Harris as soon as he drew back his hand to hit her. She'd hurt him before, and the large scar on his cheek was the result of him trying to get her to shift to human when he'd been trying to get her to come out of the cage. She'd came out all right, all teeth and claws, and nearly tore Harris apart before she'd been darted four times to knock her out.

"I want her found. She's going to play with us or I'll just kill her. She's costing me money every day that she's loose, and she is going to repay every penny of it as soon as we find her. And we will find her, won't we?" Harris nodded and stood up. "She has to be working somewhere. See if you can find someone to run her Social Security number and find her that way. If she doesn't have a job by now, she's either dead or getting paid under the table. Either way, I want to know."

After Harris left, Roy picked up the ledger again. The bear had had a good week this week and the wolves were slowly catching on to the program. Just how hard did they think this job was?

He'd been a small time thief before he'd found his first shifter. Alex Spears had even come up with the idea of him going into houses as an exotic pet and stealing from them. Roy's job had been to fence it for them. They'd split the money fifty-fifty. No one blamed the pet, and when the folks were about broke, they'd given him back his "pet." They did this for over three years when they decided to bring in other animals, ones they could control. Bear Black, his actual name, had been the first. But he'd been sloppy and had been caught. When he'd killed the couple who had him, he'd been put down before he could shift and give up what he truly was. Alex had been so scared after that that he'd wanted out.

"You have to stop this before someone else gets killed," he'd told him that night. "I can't stand the fact that this has gotten someone murdered."

"Murder is a very strong word for what happened there. And Bear is dead now and no one will ever know what we're doing." Alex was already shaking his head no. "We can slow down if it will make you feel better. Then when the news moves on to something else, we'll pick up again. In the meantime, we can gather more shifters and train them…. What are you doing?"

Alex started clearing out his desk even before Roy could try to convince him to stay. "I'm done. You can do this if you want but I'm finished with this. It was a good run, but it's over. You should get out too before it comes down on your head."

The gun was in his hand before Roy could think about it. He held it on Alex and told him to sit. When he continued to pack up his desk, Roy thought to wound him, but he'd started to shift by then and the bullet tore through his brain. He looked up at his secretary when she came rushing into the room. Her smile was a little like seeing evil spread across one's face. She looked like she was born to it.

"I guess this means you need a new partner." She slithered in. There was no other word for how she moved into the room and towards him. "I've been working on a list of my own, you see. I have a few names of others like our poor stupid shifter here that we can recruit for jobs."

She'd nearly raped him in the chair after that. He'd had her bent over his desk and fucking her as hard as he could when she begged him to slap her. He'd hit her ass when she begged him for more. Suddenly she was standing in front of him slapping him. He backhanded her once, and when she hit the floor, she came up on her knees and took him into her mouth and swallowed him. He'd never come so hard in his life. And had been enjoying her form of sex since.

He looked back on it now and realized she'd been creating tension between him and Alex for months. She'd been just waiting for this to happen, he knew now. She would probably have taken either of them at that time but he'd been the last man standing, so to speak.

She walked into his office just as if he'd conjured her up. "I've been thinking about her. Jonny is probably trying to get to her mommy and daddy. We should probably send out a little welcoming party for her if she isn't there already. They might even know where she's at, or at least heard from her."

He'd forgotten about her parents. He reached for Jonny's file to find the address when she told him. He picked up his phone and told Harris to get a few shifters out to that address as soon as possible. He hung up the phone when she started to undress.

"You should know that I have a meeting in an hour." She nodded and continued to strip. "If you want the shit beat out of you now, you're going to look like hell when our prospective clients come to call."

"So don't hit me and when we get home you can make up for it." She got down on her knees in front of him. "Or would you rather have a bite to eat first before I suck you off?"

He wanted both and told her so. But she shook her head. He watched the flare of excitement in her eyes when he hit her on the face. He ordered her to lean over his desk and when she did it, he moved his body toward her and picked up his ruler he'd bought just for her.

"I can always hurt you where they won't be able to see it. Then when I come all over your ass, you can lick me clean." She moaned and danced on her feet while opening her legs for him. "Christ, you're wet for me, aren't you? It's dripping down your legs."

Roy tore open the fly on his pants, not even bothering with taking them off. He was fisting his cock hard and using his precum to lubricate himself as he prepared her ass for him. Coming in her ass was as good as coming down her throat.

"I need you to spank me, Roy. Come on, fucking hit me." He brought the ruler down so hard it drew blood in a long cut along her ass. She cried out and begged him for more. He slammed his cock deep into her ass as he hit her three more times, each time a little harder than the last. When she came, screaming out his name, he joined her, his cock exploding into her. Before he was finished, she jerked from him and fell to her knees, taking him into her mouth as he fucked her. She came again, her eyes rolling into the back of her head as he felt his cock being strangled at the back off her throat. Christ, how did he live without her before this?

After the meeting with a couple that wanted to see if he had a leopard, he sat in his office and tried to think where he'd get one when she came back into his office. She sat in the chair opposite to him and grinned. He hated that grin.

"They told me they'd pay any price to have a leopard. Any price. They want to show it off to their friends." He watched her as she slid a piece of paper toward him.

"That's a shifter I heard of. He's in debt to his ass on gambling. I'm thinking you can buy him for the price of his debts. And since we know the man who he owes the money too, we all win."

He looked at the piece of paper before picking up the phone. "And if he won't sell us his marker, then what?"

She shrugged. "Then we kill him too."

As she moved out of the room, he shivered. Christ, she was cold. He looked at the name of the bookie and wondered why she'd say that about her own father. Anita Kidd was one cold and calculating bitch.

"Hello, Mr. Kidd. It's Roy Dawson. I was wondering if we could talk a little about Chris Reutter. I understand he owes you a great deal of money."

And just like that, he had a shifter.

~~~

Marc was in a shitty mood. Even the others in the office were steering clear of him. When he came out of his office for the second time in less than an hour to bark at someone, she slammed her desk drawer closed and stood up. She was going to lunch early and he could fuck off.

He watched her as she turned the service over, and then followed her into the little kitchen area. She was waiting for the water to boil in the microwave when he leaned against the counter beside her.

"Is that all you ever eat? Don't you crave meat or an occasional vegetable?" She didn't look at him when the machine dinged. "I'm talking to you, the least you can do is acknowledge me."

"Hello. Now get the fuck away from me. I'm on my lunch hour. My time, not yours." He growled low and her entire body went on alert; her cat seemed to skim along her skin. She stood up, dumping her lunch on the table, and backed up.

"You felt it, didn't you?" He moved toward her slowly as he spoke low. "You want to come to me, don't you? You want to touch me."
~~~

"I'm not feeling well. I would like to go home." He shook his head and continued coming toward her. "You can't keep me here. I can go when I want to."

The vending machine touched her back. She knew she was trapped. Looking to her left, she could see the wall, and to her right was another table. He was nearly to her when she looked at him. Putting out her hand made him stop, but when he took it into his hand and then to his mouth, she jerked away.

"You feel it. This attraction between us. You want me as much as I want you." She shook her head at him. "If I touch you right now, what will you do? Will I smell your arousal?"

His words were having the strangest effect on her. She tried to back further away from him as he closed the distance between them. When he ran his finger along her throat, she moaned before she could stop it. He leaned slowly into her neck and she tilted her head for him.

His tongue was hot and wet; it curved around her throat to her ear where he nipped at her lobe. Putting her hand up to push him away ended up with her curling her hand into his chest as he ran his hand down her ribs to the top of her pants. As soon as his hand touched her ribs, she moaned again. He lifted her up with his free hand and wrapped her leg over his hip. His cock rocked into her as he cupped her breast from beneath.

He touched her everywhere. His hands moved so quickly that she wasn't surprised when she felt his mouth on her nipple. He'd lifted her shirt up and her bra and was suckling hard on the tip. He tore his mouth away from her breast to take her mouth, his tongue spearing into her and dancing with her tongue like he'd been doing it forever. When he lifted her up again, this time cupping her ass, she wrapped around him and locked her ankles around him. He was fucking her through their clothes when she felt him bite gently at her shoulder. Her cat snarled at her or him, she wasn't sure which, but he bit her again, this time hard enough to make her come.

Her body was on fire now. She needed something from him, a great deal more than she was getting this way. When he stiffened and looked down at her, she could see her cat reflected back at her. Or was it? She heard someone coming and tried to struggle free of him. He leaned to her ear and nipped before speaking.

"It's Dennis. He's not coming in here but going out. Just be quiet and he'll be gone soon." He licked along her throat again. "As much as I would love to finish this, we have to talk."

Finish? She looked down at herself and closed her eyes. She was half-naked in an office with her boss. A boss she didn't really like. She grabbed her shirt and pulled it back over her. He let her go when she unhooked her legs from him and turned around to finish putting her clothes to right. His chuckle made her turn around.

"This isn't funny. I would very much like it if you'd step back. I want to…." She wanted to have him lay her across the table and take her, but knew that wasn't the best course of action to take. When he put his arms over his chest and smiled at her, she found she wanted to hit him hard enough to knock him across the room, but found she couldn't.

"You're not going anywhere until we have a talk. I want you to come into my office, I'll order us a big lunch and we'll discuss what's going to happen now." He reached for her hand and she shoved both of them behind her. "You have to know that things between us are different now. I've marked you."

She didn't know what that meant, and was pretty sure she didn't want to know either. When he reached for her again, she flinched away from his touch. She saw the hurt flare in his eyes and felt a moment of regret for causing it, but she had to get away from him and think. She said the first thing that came to her.

"You have to leave me alone. I'm not what you think I am." He grinned bigger and nodded. "I mean I'm a woman like you see, but there's more to me than you see. And I'm being followed. You can't want to get involved even if it's just a one night fuck because these people will hurt anyone they think are close to me."

"Does it have anything to do with the fact that you're a panther?" Her body froze and her blood felt as if it stopped flowing through her body. He touched the place where he'd bitten her and ran his finger over her breast to her heart. It seemed to skip several beats as he watched her.

"I don't know what you're talking about." He nodded once and touched his mouth to hers gently. "You have to stop doing that. I have…I have a husband and he won't be happy when I tell him what you're doing."

"You're not married. In fact, you've never been with a man before. I can smell your virginity on you like a sweet wine." His mouth moved up her chin to her lips, where he suckled the lower one into his mouth before he continued. "You have no idea how much I'm going to enjoy making you mine."

She felt her cat purr and he raised his head to look at her. She had to get away from him, now before it was too late. Jonny shoved at him and he took a step back, then another. She moved toward the door and he followed her, not touching her again.

"I'm not feeling well. I have to go home and…." She grabbed up her bag and put it on her shoulder. She felt as if she wasn't really there, that someone else had taken over her body and was speaking for her. She turned to look at him, unsure why she wanted him to take her into his arms.

"You can't hide from me now. If you don't come to work tomorrow I will find you, and if there's anything that even resembles a bed, I'm going to take you on it. You're safer here at work, where I can't do all the things I want to do to you because of the people here. Do you understand what I'm telling you?"

She nodded, then shook her head. "You're scaring me. I don't know what's going on, but you're scaring me."

"I know, love, and I'm sorry for that, but I didn't know. I thought once was the only chance I'd ever get." He walked her to the elevator. "May I kiss you again?"

He didn't really wait for her to answer, which she supposed was a good thing. He took her mouth in the most amazing, gentle kiss she'd had. But then she hadn't had that many to begin with. When he stepped back, she entered the elevator, and he stopped the doors before they closed.

"Your real name, what is it?" She shook her head and stepped further into the cubical. "No matter, you'll give it to me soon enough after you learn to trust me."

She was nearly a block from her apartment when she realized she had gone that far. She moved into the first store she saw and watched the street. She hadn't been paying attention, and that would get her killed.

When no one seemed to be watching, she walked around the store again just to make sure. When the clerk looked at her for the second time, she purchased the first thing she touched and put it on the counter. He smiled at her when she realized what she'd bought.

"That one is pretty reliable. My girlfriend and I use it all the time. I suppose one of these times we're going to get caught, but it's a good pregnancy test." He asked her if she wanted a bag and she nodded, mortified.

She stuffed it into her bag and left, this time more alert than before. She was just rounding the corner to her apartment when she saw him. It took her a few seconds to remember if he'd been someone from the office or from the house. When she remembered his name, her skin grew clammy and she backed against the building. She was sure he'd not seen her, but she was still afraid. She watched him move to a car. He drove down the street before she moved again. It was time to go. They were too close for her to live there any longer.

CHAPTER 6

Marc waited for her to come out of the building for ten minutes. He wished he'd realized sooner that she lived there, but he'd been so wrapped up in not believing she was his mate and hadn't bothered to look into where she was or even how close she was. Her fear had made him move toward her to find her. Dumb luck had him in the alley when she'd gone into the building at the basement level. He pulled out his key to open the door when she didn't come out after ten minutes.

The entire first floor looked like she'd never been through there. He looked at the stairs and noticed right away that she'd gone that way, but she'd been careful to step on the carpet and not the wood on either side. Even the cobwebs hadn't been disturbed. He moved up to the second floor and noticed the same thing. He looked up the stairs to the third floor, where he heard her talking. He wondered if she was alone, and realized she was. There were no other scents in the stairwell but hers.

This part of the building was vastly different than the rooms below. She'd cleaned it, and it nearly sparkled. He looked in the kitchen and saw that she had two more boxes of the noodles on the counter, and there was a single plate and fork on a clean towel on the counter. He moved toward where she was, pulling his gun just in case. She was stuffing clothes into her backpack when he saw her.

He had expected her to be on the defense, but her shifting from human to cat startled him, especially how smoothly she did it. He didn't move as she looked at him, a low growl coming from her throat. He slowly put his gun away, stepped into the room, and closed the door. If she wanted to, she would be able to break it down, but he was hoping to get to talk to her before she wanted to run again.

"You're a beautiful panther. I knew you would be the moment I saw you." She snarled at him and circled around him as he moved closer to her. "I knew you were a cat, you see, even if you didn't tell me. I could smell you as one of my own kind."

She stopped moving and sat down. He didn't think she was willing to listen, because her fur was still standing at her neck and her claws had not retracted. He sat down on the floor and held his hands in front of him as he talked to her.

"I bit you. Do you know what that means?" She shook her head. "I didn't think you did. You seem to be very uninformed about what you are and knowing who the others are around you. It means I've marked you as my mate. I took your blood. That's how I knew to come looking for you. I could sense your fear."

She looked out the window and then back at him. He supposed that he could have moved toward her, but thought she'd have his throat ripped out before he could shift to bring her down. Besides, he wanted her trust more than anything.

"You're being chased by someone. He wants you because you're a cat, right?" She lay down but didn't answer him. He was okay with that for now. He reached out to her mind and connected with her.

Would you rather talk to me this way? She lifted her head and growled low. *I want to speak to you, and if you won't shift, this is the best way. I'm not here to hurt you but to protect you.*

I don't want your protection. I don't need it. She looked at her bag, then back at him. *I have to change and you're keeping me from being able to.*

I'm not leaving you. You can either shift with me here or I shift with you and we sit here all night. Either way, I'm not leaving you until we figure out together what's happening.

She really was a beautiful woman and a gorgeous cat. He smiled at her and stretched out his legs as he started talking to her. She laid her head down and watched him. Marc had a feeling it was going to be a long night.

As my mate, you and I are connected on a level that no other animal or human can breach. We'll be able to communicate no matter the distance. You can't block me from speaking to you nor finding you. The same applies toward me. Especially when you're afraid like you were before. What scared you? He didn't expect her to answer, so he wasn't surprised when she didn't. *I'm assuming that it has to do with Roy Dawson and his animals. Does he want you for breeding purposes, or something else?*

He'd seen her stiffen and knew that she was afraid of the man. He was going to tell her how he'd found out the man's name when she spoke finally. He didn't move as she started telling him things he couldn't believe of a human being.

He has a bunch of people like me. Well, not any of them are like me, I'm the only panther. He sells us to people who want an exotic animal in their homes. She'd said *sell* like it was a dirty word. *When we get into the house we're supposed to case the place and report back to him what we've found. He tells us what to steal, and he comes to collect it where he tells us to leave it.*

And you were a part of this bunch? She nodded. *How long did you work for him before you escaped?*

A month. He had my friend, Anita Kidd. He said that he would kill her if I didn't do what he wanted of me. That once I was in the house and got him what he wanted from the family, he'd let her go, and me. But he lied to me, so I told him that he had to let us go. When he didn't, I made my own arrangements. That's when I saw him kill her as I was leaving to find her. He killed her while they were in his bedroom.

He didn't think that sounded right but didn't comment. He watched her as she got up to move back and forth in front of him. Marc had no idea why but he had a feeling she had forgotten about him in favor of the memory she was having.

I don't know though. It sounded like her, but.... She looked at him as he shifted his legs again, but again he had the feeling she wasn't see him. *She wasn't very upset with him, not like I thought she'd be for being tied up. She'd sounded like...almost like she'd been reading from a script. Him too. I wonder now if they had been practicing for this moment, like they knew at some point that I'd have to see this.*

Why? She looked at him this time, really looked. *Why do you think they were practicing? What did you hear or see that made you think that? Tell me, Joan, don't think just say it.*

She was laughing when I climbed out the window and left. I heard her laughter. She looked at him, confused. *Dead women don't laugh.*

She lay down again and watched him. He didn't try to fill the silence with small talk and was pretty sure she'd not tolerate it if he did. Instead, he let her think about whatever it was she was thinking about while he watched her. After an hour or so she finally spoke again.

I would like to shift now. If you'll just step outside I won't be able to leave. I can't stay this way for very long or I won't be able to shift back. He started to tell her that was an old wives tale but didn't. If she shifted they could leave here soon and he could take her to his house. He nodded and stood up and walked to the door. Before he stepped through it, he turned back to her.

"Joan, will you tell me your real name now?" She watched him for long moments before she answered him. He thanked her and moved out of the room so she could change, and he contacted Khan.

I need you to find out all you can about theft's concerning homes with exotic pets and anything you can find on Jonny Thomas. He repeated it twice more so that Khan could write it down. *She's coming to my house for now, and I'll bring her to you sometime in the next few days.*

She trusts you then? Good. We can't help her if she won't let us. How did you get her to open up? You didn't fuck her into submission, did you? Khan's laughter pissed him off a little, and he had to take a couple of short breaths so he wouldn't snarl at him.

She's my mate. I just figured it out today. That shut him up quickly. He waited for Khan to say something, anything, but he didn't. Marc closed off the connection as soon as he heard Jonny moving toward him.

~~~

She let him lead her to his car. It wasn't that she was giving into him, she was just beaten. When he turned onto the main highway, she looked at him. She tried to think her best way out of town.

"I think the best solution is for you to take me to the bus station. I'm pretty sure I have enough money for a ticket to somewhere. I've about four thousand dollars." He glanced at her but didn't say anything. "I have some money here that I'd like you to give to the owner of the building I was using. I'm not sure how much rent it is but I—"

"I own the buildings on either side of me. I bought them several years ago with plans of turning them into offices. I just never got around to it." She nodded and reached into her bag to get his money. "And I'm not taking your money, so if that's what you're reaching for, you might as well put it back."

"But I lived there for almost two months without paying for anything. I'm not a mooch. I already paid the man I took the clothes from. He didn't seem to have any problems taking my money."

"Did he know you took the clothes and then eventually paid him back?" She shook her head. "Well I do, and I'm not taking it. Also, just to give you a heads up, I own The Vintage Shoppe too. And I'm not taking you to the bus station."

She looked out the window and wondered how much a plane ticket was going to cost her when he drove past that exit too. Jonny turned in her seat and looked at him. He was driving her nuts.
~~~

"I demand that you pull over this minute and let me out. I thought you were going to help me get away. They're close, and if you're with me, he might do something stupid and…." Something he'd said at the apartment occurred to her. "You said I didn't recognize that we were the same. What did you mean by that?"

"Just what you think it means. I'm a panther too. My entire family is. My parents were full-bloods, and so each of us boys is as well." He glanced at her. "I don't know that you're a full-blood, but you're very close. Are your parents both panthers?"

"Neither of them is. I think maybe I was adopted, but I never asked and they never treated me like I was anything but theirs. Then when I was thirteen, I became this thing and they still loved me." She watched the trees fly by as he got off the highway and onto a street. "I haven't seen them in five months. I was afraid that Roy will go and hurt them to get me to come to them."

"Where do they live?" She told him that it wasn't any of his business. "I can go and bring them to my house so they'll be safe. You have to trust me."

"No, I don't." She picked up her bag when he put on his turn signal on. She was ready to take off, but once she saw the large gates open, then close behind them, she turned to him. This was getting to be too much.

When the car stopped, he grabbed her arm and held her. He was much stronger than her, and he held her until she stopped struggling. He didn't let her go, but he did loosen his hand enough that it didn't hurt.

"You're going to come into my house, and we're going to sit down and have a nice conversation. We're going to go over all the information you have about Dawson, and then we're going to—"

"You're going to fuck me, aren't you? Whether or not I want to, you're going to finish what you started at the apartment." He let her go and stared at her for several seconds before he got out of the car. When he came around to her side, she thought he was going to jerk her out, but he opened the door and held out his hand to her. She felt foolish and childish. When she took his hand, he helped her out and reached in for her bag. When she started to demand that he return it, he simply handed it to her. He pressed her to the car gently and looked down at her.

"I don't rape women. I especially wouldn't rape you. You'd kill me before I got my pants down." His lips twitched and she watched them as he continued. "I'm your mate, and as such, I don't want to do anything but cherish you."

She licked her lips, thinking about his being on hers. The way he'd suckled at her breast and bitten her. When he growled low, she looked into his eyes and saw his cat just there on the surface. Her entire body heated in response.

"I can smell you, your arousal. Do you know what that does to me? To my cat?" She nodded. "I guess you do. I want you, Jonny. I could take you right here if you'd let me."

He rocked into her, and she moaned. Shifting his body, she opened her legs so that he could be closer to her heat. When he rocked into her again, she dug her nails into his shoulders to hang on.

His mouth slid over his bite from earlier and she felt her cat stir. When he lifted his head from her shoulder, she watched him as he cupped her ass and pulled her up to his hips. His cock was pressed hard into her soft folds, and she wanted more of him.

"Say it." She trembled at his words as he growled them at her. "Tell me, Jonny. Tell me what you want."

She locked her heels behind him and curled her fingers into his shirt collar. Watching him, she tore it from him, baring his chest for her to touch. When she lowered her head to his nipple to bite him, he jerked her head up by her hair and held her.

It seemed like they were at battle. She didn't want to say she wanted him, and he needed her to say it. She knew it was because of what she'd said to him about raping her, but she was afraid if she gave him permission for this, it would never be the same, she'd never be able to leave him. When he lowered his head again and licked at the scar he'd branded her with, her body clenched tight, ready for him to sink his teeth into her again. But he lifted his head and watched her. She was so close, so very close to losing it all that she nearly said no.

"Yes. Please, take me." His mouth was brutal as he took it. When he lifted her from the car, she held onto him as he struggled to get his keys out of his pockets. His shirt in tatters around his arms hung on at his wrist with his cufflinks, his tie still clung to his neck. As soon as the door opened he took her to the table and swiped everything on it to the floor. Her back touched the hard surface even as the last cup shattered.

Her clothes fared no better than his had. Her shirt was torn away, then her bra. His claws skimmed along her skin and brought goose bumps as he cut though her pants. Before she could protest, even if she had wanted to, she was lying on his table, naked but for her panties.

"Christ, you're more beautiful than I ever thought you'd be." He tore out his links and tossed them behind him. When he reached for his belt, she sat up and ripped it from him by opening the button and jerking them off. He stood before her in his boxers and nothing else.

Marc ran his hands down her ribs and up under her breasts. Slowly, he explored her, touching her here then moving to another part of her to touch and soothe her there. He watched her face, and when she closed her eyes, overwhelmed by the sensations, he stopped.

"I'm going to taste you. I want to…." He took a deep breath as he ran his fingers across her soaking panties. "You're so wet for me that I could slide into you without any problems. But you're a virgin and I want to make this good for you before I have to hurt you."

"I don't care. Please just take me, Marc." He shook his head and grabbed a chair and sat it between her legs. Then he sat down. She tried to close her legs, but he wouldn't let her. Instead, he widened them until she felt completely exposed.

He tore her panties away, her last barrier between them. As he lowered his head, she felt herself get wetter and tried to close her legs again. This time he held her the way he wanted her but curling his hands over her thighs. She felt his breath on her and shivered.

"You smell delicious. I'm going to enjoy this very much." His tongue teased her clit, and she cried out. Her body seemed poised on a ledge, and she knew he was going to push her off. As soon as his mouth covered her, she felt his finger enter her. Jonny wanted more and less at the same time. She wanted him to make her fall, but she was afraid of hitting the ground when he did. But when he suckled her clit into his mouth and nipped at her, suddenly she didn't care what he did to her.

Her first climax tore from her. His mouth and tongue were driving her higher and higher, only to let her down again. It took her breath away one minute how close she was until he moved and her body fell back. She reached down and grabbed his hair and tried to guide him back to where she wanted, but he laughed and lifted his head.

"You come once more for me baby, and I'll give you what we both want. But I want you to come hard, no holding back. I want to feel you come around my mouth and drink deeply from you. All right?"

She begged him, pleaded with him to give her what she wanted now, but he only lowered his head and licked her. When he entered her again, she felt his fingers move, dig, and pull at her. When he touched something in her, she cried out and heard him chuckle. He was relentless after that. His mouth and fingers brought her closer and closer until she was dizzy from need. When he slid his finger up her ass, she tensed for a second. Then he slowly rubbed his thumb over her tight muscles. Every swipe brought her closer still until he pressed inside at the same moment he bit her clit.

She screamed. Her body didn't just fall over the edge but leapt over. Every time she felt herself ready to land, he'd nip again and move deeper into her bottom. There was a pain, short and over before she could voice it. Then he was standing over her, his cock fisted in his hand. She sat up and reached for him.

He closed his hand over hers as she held his cock. "You do that and I'm going to come all over you instead of inside of you. And while that sounds wonderful, I want to feel you wrapped around me."

She nodded and lay back. Marc held himself as he moved his thick cock at her entrance. She moaned each time he touched her sensitive clit. When his head breached her pussy, she moaned and arched up.

"Now, Marc, Christ now." He slammed deep and she felt his balls at her ass. Every part of her screamed to tell him to stop, to pull out of her because it hurt too much. But she lay very still, as still as he was.

"I'm going to move slowly, love. I've already taken your maidenhead, but I have to mark you again." She shifted and moaned. "Christ, baby, if you do that again I'm not going to be able to go slow."

She moved again and felt his cock move into her deeper. She watched him as he held himself over her, and noticed that he looked to be in pain. Sweat beaded on his forehead, and she reached up to touch him. He kissed her palm as he moved slowly.

"You're so beautiful. And mine. All mine." His words, softly spoken, seemed to touch her deeper than he was, touch her in ways she knew that meant everything. As he moved in and out of her, she wrapped her legs around his hips. He leaned over her, his mouth inches from her.

When he kissed her it was gentle and soft, his body covered her from breast to hips, and still it felt as if he was everywhere. As soon as his mouth moved to her shoulder again, she licked her lips. She wanted to bite him as badly as she wanted him to bite her. When he licked along her shoulder, she did the same to his. His body shuddered over hers, and he moved faster. Wanting him to bite her, needing for him to, she was startled when her release took her; it came over her like a fast moving storm, completely obliterating everything from her mind but what she was feeling. As soon as he stiffened above her, she pulled him closer and sank her teeth into his muscle, tearing it open so that blood filled her mouth. Her second climax hit her when he bit her, his roar muffled by his bite.

CHAPTER 7

Khan sat in the chair after talking to Marc for the longest time. He wasn't sure what to think or do. His brother had a mate. Marc had a chance at happiness. But Khan was afraid.

"Why?" He looked up at his own mate. "You said you were afraid for him, why? Don't you want him to be happy?"

"Of course I do. What a thing to say." He stood up and got them both glasses and then the tea. "I'm just worried that…. What if she's not really his mate and he just wants her to be? Where will he be then if he's loved twice and he loses them both?"

"What a horrible thing to say," his mom said, entering the room. He looked at her. "I was with Marc the other day, and let me tell you, young man, she's his mate even if you don't believe it."

"I didn't say I didn't believe it. I only said I was worried that he might want it so badly that he thinks she's his mate. We all remember how hard he took it when Sonya was killed. Christ, Mom, I don't want to see him go through that again."

"She's his mate. And when you see them together you'll believe it too. He just needs to claim her and it'll all be right there where you can see it." He flushed when his mom glared at him. "What is it, Khan? What do you know?"

"He wanted me to find out about her parents. I did and…. I talked to him a few minutes ago. Her parents aren't panthers. They're humans. He said that Jonny—his mate's real name is Jonny Thomas—he said that she is worried that they'll use them to get to her."

"What are we going to do to get them to safety? I'm assuming you and Marc mean to bring them here." He nodded at Monica. "Well, what's the plan, big boy? Don't leave us in the dark."

"Caitlynne is fixing it now. She's taking Dylan, and she wants you to go as well. But I don't—"

"If you say you aren't going to let me, you'd better have a damned good reason why I should allow you to live." Monica crossed her arms over her breasts and stared at him. "I mean it, Khan. I'm not going to stand by when I can be helpful."

"I didn't say you couldn't go. I just wish you wouldn't." He loved his mate very much, but she was very strong minded. When she grinned at him, Khan knew that she'd heard his thoughts.

"Caitlynne will get them here. And I'm betting the bad guys won't even know it." His mom sat sandwiches in front of Monica and him. "And don't think because I love this idea that I'm not still mad at you about my house and car."

Khan nodded and smiled to himself. She may be acting all pissy about it, but he knew she was having fun with the decorators. He loved having her and Dad at his house too. Maybe too much; he was worried about what the contractors were going to say tomorrow when he met with them. The house was getting very old and somewhat unsafe.

His house phone rang and he got up to answer it. He turned to look at Monica when she asked him who it was. He told her it was Caitlynne.

"I have things on this end set up. And Dylan is going to meet me at the airport in two hours. Can you have Monica there?" He told her that he could. "She's going to be our secondary man, so she'll be very safe. I just need two medics on the team, and she's going to be controlling Mr. Thomas."

"Controlling him? I don't understand. Why do you need him to be controlled?" He looked at Monica. "I don't like this, Caitlynne. If you're going to get my mate hurt, you—"

"I won't, and I need her to control John because he's going to be dead."

Khan was nervous to be staying at home with Jonny, but he promised his brother that he'd keep her safe. And her going could be a problem on the other end. He glanced at her as the car left the drive.

"They'll be fine. Caitlynne is very good at her job." Jonny nodded and walked away toward the living room. Khan thought it might be a good time to get to know her a little better while his family was gone and his mom and dad were with the children, his and Walker's. He sat down beside her on the couch.

"Can you give me a little more information on what Dawson had you do in the house when you got inside? I mean, what sort of stuff did he have you steal?" She glanced at him, then back at the fire. "I'm guessing that only the very wealthy can afford exotic animals."

"He had a profile on them before we had to go in." Her voice was clipped, but he had been told by Marc that she still didn't trust him completely.

"I would imagine he has people doing that for him. I wonder how much that would cost. I would suppose it would be worth it if the jewels and stuff were high priced enough. Could be—"

"I'm not going to do it." He looked at her, confused. "I'm not going to pretend to be an animal so I can rob your friend's houses. I didn't want to do it for him, and I most certainly won't do it for you. Find another way to make some quick bucks. I'm not helping."

Anger surged through him, and he stood when she did. "Sit down." His voice was full of compulsion, and she fought it, but in the end sat. He took several deep breaths before he spoke, but she did first.

"I don't know what you just did to me, but you'll not do it again. I'm not a child to be ordered around like I'm stupid. I also won't be a thief, not for anyone."

"If you don't want to be treated as a child, then stop acting like one. I asked you a question to try and figure out an angle on making this person pay for what he's done to you and others. I don't need to rob other people's homes, and if that was my plan, I could simply shift into a bigger cat and do it myself." She glanced at him. "Look at me, Jonny, please."

She looked at him for a second, then away. He knew she'd look back, and he waited. When she did, he held her chin as he looked into her eyes. She was in pain and a great deal of it. She'd been abused and threatened since she'd been a child. The only people she trusted at all were her parents. He let her go when she pulled back.

"Marc said you don't know a great deal about your own kind," he said. "He said that you have very little knowledge about what you really are as well." She didn't answer, but then he didn't think she would admit to not knowing something. "I can answer any questions you have. I'm sure there are going to be plenty over the next few years. Do you understand that you and Marc are mates?"

"He told me. I don't know why he wants me, but he seems to." She glanced at him again. "I don't want him to get hurt."

"He won't, not with all the rest of them there. Caitlynne is my sister-in-law, yours too, I suppose, in a way. She'll kick his ass if he gets hurt. She's somewhat of a pain in my ass, but I don't have to live with her. Walker does." He'd tried for a joke, but it failed miserably. "Marc is a good man. He'll protect you."

"I don't really need him to protect me. I've been doing just fine on my own." He raised a brow at her. "Okay, I really haven't, but it wasn't for lack of trying. I was doing all right."

"You kept yourself alive, that's a plus." She snorted and he laughed. "My mom does that too. She is gonna love you. And my dad…you should ask someone before you believe anything he tells you. He doesn't really lie so much as he likes to stir up trouble."

"I don't know how to love people without getting them hurt." She moved to the floor and in front of the fireplace. "When they took me away from my house when I turned fifteen, I thought I'd never see my parents again. Then when I escaped, I stupidly went back home. Roy caught me in days."

"He knew you'd go where you felt safe." She nodded. "What did he do to you? And how long did he have you?"

"The second time he had me for three years. I would get away, but he'd catch me pretty quick. He made me believe that I was the only one of my kind. The only panther in the world that could be a girl as well as this thing I am." She shifted on the floor again before she continued. "The third time he had me was when I was nineteen. He held me in a cell for almost a year before he'd let me out. I suppose it was because I kicked his ass and mopped up the floor with him. He…he beat me and tossed me in there. I thought for sure he'd forgotten about me. But he hadn't."

Khan tried to imagine what it would be like to be locked in a cell for a year. Before he'd met Monica he had been locked in this house, hiding from the world, but his family had come by to make sure he was all right. She'd had no one.

"I was able to escape again. I'd…I had to hurt someone to get out. I wish it had been Roy but it was one of his minions. I hated myself for it until I realized that he would have hurt me without any problems."

"You killed him, didn't you?" They both looked at his mom when she spoke. "You had to kill him to get free, didn't you?"

"Yes. I didn't mean to. But I had no control over the cat, and he attacked me. I shifted and tore his throat out before I could stop the monster inside of me."

"You're not a monster, Jonny. You're a predator, yes, and one that kills to survive, just like the rest of us. But you're not a monster." Khan looked at his mom when she sat next to Jonny as he continued. "My mom is a panther. Does she look like a monster to you?"

Jonny stared at her for a few seconds. He wasn't sure what was going through her head, but he would bet it was a horrific memory. When she spoke, it was as soft as a whimper from his child in his sleep.

"Have you killed to survive, Mrs. Bowen?" His mom had, and he knew it. When she nodded at Jonny, the girl looked at him. He nodded as well.

Jonny nodded. She looked so lost and so hurt that Khan, not usually a man who hugged a stranger, wanted to pull her into his lap and hold her as he would his own children. She sat there staring at the fire until his dad came into the room. His dad was the greatest man he knew. But there were times….

"So, who died?" His voice thundered across the room, and he smiled at Jonny. "Christ, you're a pretty little thing, aren't you?"

"Dad, this is Jonny Thomas. She's going to be staying with us until Marc returns with her parents." He nodded at him but stared at Jonny. "Dad?"

"You're related to Deb Anderson, aren't you?" Jonny shook her head. "Yeah, you might not know it, but she's probably your mom. Her mate…what was his name?" He turned to Khan's mom when he asked.

"Travis? You mean Travis Anderson? I thought he was dead," Khan said. His dad nodded, and his mom nodded too. "They had a baby. A little girl that…. Deb said she died, that the baby died at birth."

They all looked at her, and Jonny squirmed. Khan knew how she felt. They were looking at her like she was a spec on a microscope glass. His dad finally got up and reached for her hand.

"I just asked Marc if I could touch you. He said that I was to explain to you what I mean. He said that you wouldn't understand." Jonny shook her head. "He's marked you, honey, as his own, and when another male touches what is his, he can be a little…." He looked at Khan.

"We can be a little mad, as in violent, about it and want to mark you again and kill the other male. He gave Dad permission so he won't kill him, but…well, he'll mark you again so you no longer smell like another male."

"That's the stupidest thing I've ever heard." They all looked at each other and not her. "And marking? You mean…."

He nodded at her. Her face couldn't have gotten any redder, he was sure. When his dad laughed, she glared at him.

"You can be mad all you want, child, but it's the way we are. Kind of on the possessive side, we males are. You, too, if he comes back smelling like another female. Turned don't have that same instinct as purebloods. You'll see when he comes back if you don't smell another female on him."

"George, you're embarrassing her. Stop before I show you how pissy a full-blood can be." Khan was embarrassed and wanted them to simply stop, but his mom changed the subject. "You have your permission. Now touch her before I have to smack that stupid smile off your face."

His dad was still laughing when he put his hand on her cheek. When he ran it over her throat, Jonny flinched away. His dad winked at her and sat back. He looked both smug and upset about whatever it was he found.

"You're their daughter. I can…it's been a long while, but I can still feel another cat's sires. One of my gifts."

She looked at the fire, then back at him. Even Khan could see the tears in her eyes.

"I don't know them. Do you know…do I want to know why they gave me up?" His dad shrugged and told her he could find out for her. "I'd like that, please. I don't know where I'll be, but I'll be more than glad to call you sometime."

"Where are you going, child?" His mom asked before he could. "You and Marc will stay here in his home. I hadn't heard that he was leaving, had you, Khan?"

He started to say he didn't think that's what she meant when she spoke again. There were times when he wished he wasn't the leader and didn't have to be the bearer of bad news.

"You can't leave him, Jonny. You and he are connected now and considered one. If you leave him or try to leave him, he'll just find you and bring you back." She stood up to pace, and he found himself relieved that she wasn't going to hurt him. Yet.

"And I get no say in this? How is that even lawful?" His dad laughed, and she glared at him. "Laugh it up, buddy, and I touch you without his permission."

His mom burst out laughing when his dad's mouth snapped closed. "Oh, I like you. You're going to do just fine with this family. Come along, dear; let's go into the kitchen and let these two wonder what we're going to poison them with. Have you ever heard what saltpeter does to a male? You should hear what it does to a panther."

He looked at his dad as he watched the women go into the kitchen. There was something very frightening about two women talking about your demise. His dad slowly turned to him.

"You really don't think they'd do that, do you?" Khan looked at the kitchen door, then back as his dad and shrugged. "Maybe we could just order in. That way we could give them a…a break from cooking? Do you know if Jonny can even cook?"

"I don't know if she's ever even been in a kitchen before this." Khan stood up, then sat back down. "We should go in and help. I can cut things up for them."

His dad nodded, and they both stood again. "Course, they could be kidding. We could just be putting ourselves out there to have to help in the kitchen more often."

Khan nodded. Yes, they could be. But there was something bigger going on here, and he grinned at his dad.

"Could be, but that would mean that they didn't kill us. Sorry, Dad, but I like that a hell of a lot better than *not* having to help out in the kitchen once in a while because I'm dead."

His dad nodded and followed him. "Yeah, I do want to live a while longer. And if we show them that we're willing to let this go, then maybe they—"

"Dad, why don't you let me do the talking? I'm pretty sure that you'll get all of us murdered in our sleep or enough saltpeter in our food to make it difficult for us for some time to come." Khan winced at his poor choice of words as did his dad. "I'm gonna help."

As they walked to the kitchen, his dad patted him on the back. "Good thing you're leader, son, I'd hate to have to deal with Marc when he comes back and he finds out I touched his mate."

He stopped moving forward and his dad bumped into him. "You said you talked to him. You said you got permission."

"Well, I knew he was busy and I got some information that we didn't have before. I don't think he'll mind overly much."

Khan had a feeling his brother was going to mind a great deal. His dad might have just started a war, and probably knew it, too. They walked into the kitchen. His dad then started telling his mom and Jonny that he'd come up with a brilliant plan and they were ordering in. Khan sat at the table and tried to figure out how to keep Marc from killing him and their father.

CHAPTER 8

Marc wasn't thrilled with the plan, but Caitlynne assured him that simple was better. He hoped the hell so, because this one was as simple as it got. He walked to the next house, two before the Thomas household, and this time Dylan knocked. When the door opened, he went into his practiced spiel.

"Hello, we're in the neighborhood today selling magazine subscriptions. We were wondering if you had a moment that we could—"

The door slammed in his face this time. "At least you got to speak. Last three times I didn't even get 'hello' out before they were slamming the door. And that other woman…sheesh, Dylan, what the fuck?"

She'd let them in and then proceeded to try and seduce them. She'd gone into the kitchen to get them a drink and had come back fucking naked. Marc shivered again. He looked at Dylan as he laughed.

"She was something. I never meet this kind of interesting people as a teacher. Of course, I do run into an occasional mother who wants to up her kid's grade by blowing me, but I can't say that any of them came to a parent-teacher meeting buck-assed naked."

The next house brought them to the neighbor of the Thomases. They knocked and waited and Marc looked around. Caitlynne had told them that there were two cars on the street that didn't belong there and she had a hit on one of them, as he was the grandson of one of the residents. The other was coming back as a rental car.

"It could be nothing, but I'm thinking that rental cars don't usually have two people sitting in them for eight hours at a time before someone else comes to sit in it. Those men are who we're watching." Caitlynne had told them this as she put bulletproof vests on them under their jackets. "Just in case."

He'd worn them before, but this seemed more…scary. He hoped to Christ that the Thomases were home. He heard a small ding in his ear before Caitlynne spoke to them. The earpieces had been her idea to keep in contact with them.

"There are two people in the house. One in the kitchen and one in the upper room. Probably the bathroom, as it seems to be in the center of the house." Marc heard the door in front of him open as Caitlynne continued. "I'm contacting Jonny now to get her ready to call if they need her to confirm you're who you say. Stay with the program, guys, or they could be tipped off."

He said "hello," and the door slammed in their faces. He took in a slow breath and let it out as the moved to the next house. He had his clipboard ready, and when he knocked on the door, Dylan said he was ready. As soon as the door opened, Dylan touched the hand of the woman standing there.

"Hello, we're in the neighborhood selling magazine subscriptions and wondered if you had a few moments that we could talk to you. Here is what we're offering today."

She took the clipboard just as who Marc assumed was John Thomas came down the stairs. Dylan put out his hand, and the man took it automatically. The woman paled when she read the note on the pad he'd handed her.

"May we come in?" She nodded at them and handed the clipboard to the man behind her. As soon as the door shut behind him and Dylan, Marc put his finger to his lips and handed them a second note. He took the first one that said, *Jonny is safe and with us. She wants us to bring you to her. Let us in.*

The second note was a little more detailed. *Don't say a word about what we're doing here. We have a plan that will get you both out safely, but you have to trust us.*

Mrs. Thomas, Erma, nodded and sat down. "What sort of magazines are you selling? I must confess…." Her voice stammered a little as she continued. "I must confess it's been a long while since I've read one."

Marc nodded. He handed her a notepad and pen. Dylan spoke to John as Marc talked to Erma. Both of them were doing a great job, and he thought he knew where Jonny got her integrity.

Is she all right? He nodded at the note. *Those men came here two days ago. Are you with them?* He shook his head and wrote his own note.

I'm her mate. Do you know what that means? Erma nodded. *She's safe at my brother's house. Would you like to go there?*

She nodded and wiped at her tears. He nodded and took the notepad from her. *Pack only what you can't live without. Once you're both gone they will destroy whatever you left behind. Do you have a fireproof safe that you can store valuables in for now?*

She nodded and pointed to the floor. She stood up and announced she was going to make some tea, would they like any per the script he'd handed her. Both he and Dylan told her yes. John watched his wife move up the stairs, and Marc handed him the note he'd given his wife.

While they were both upstairs, Dylan went to the kitchen and Marc sat in the living room reading the script. It was boring and long and told about each of the magazines that they were supposed to be selling. Dylan came in twice to read his part but for the most part Marc was alone while Dylan made noises in the kitchen like he was brewing up some tea. When the Thomases came down with three suitcases, he nodded for them to sit.

"Do you have any questions?" The last note he handed to John when he asked the two at the bottom of the paper. He looked up after reading it and smiled. The man was going to be just fine. Marc followed him into the kitchen, where he was going to hit him.

John braced himself against the counter. When he closed his eyes, Marc decided that this was by and far the hardest thing he'd ever done. Drawing back his fist, he hit the man and let him fall to the floor. As he tumbled forward, he grabbed onto the plates that had been on the counter and took them with him. Marc hurried back to the living room.

"John? Are you all right?" Erma went into the kitchen and screamed. She picked up her phone and Marc handed her the phone number. She screamed in the phone that her husband had fallen and he wasn't breathing. Caitlynne, on the other end of the call, told her that they'd send an ambulance right away.

Five minutes later, their ambulance pulled up. Monica got out of the back, along with Walker, and Reed stood by the ambulance with the doors opened. And just like Caitlynne had said, every neighbor on the street came out to see what was going on.

When John was brought out of the house on a stretcher, Marc helped Erma into the back with her husband. In the cases that the "medics" loaded was everything they had packed. Walker was with John as Monica came out with the last of the equipment. Marc stood by, panicky, when one of the men from the car approached her.

"What happened? Is he dead?" She bumped against him and looked up at him. "He's dead, and the woman might be having a heart attack too."

Monica looked over at him and winked. She'd just made the man from the car believe that John was dead and that Erma might be close behind. He nearly laughed out loud, but just barely managed to stop it. When they drove off, the ding in his ear sounded.

"Now, if you and Dylan would be so kind, I'd very much be happy if you got the fuck out of there before someone notices that you're still hanging around. Simply walk to the next street over, and, if no one is following you, I'll pick you up."

"And if there is someone following us?" he asked her. He heard her laughter before she spoke.

"Then I'm afraid you're royally fucked." Marc decided that he didn't much care for his sister-in-law at that moment and thought that if he ever got the chance, he was going to get back at her. Grinning, he thought that he'd most definitely live longer if he just let it go. Besides, she'd done him a huge favor today, and he always paid his debt.

~~~

She was sitting in the big overstuffed chair, reading a book to one of the children, when Corrine came back into
~~~

the room. She looked so excited that Jonny didn't ask who was on the phone when it was handed to her. She said hello and waited for someone to speak.

"Jonny? It's Mom, love. We're safe. He got us out, we're coming to you." Jonny sat up in the chair, completely forgetting about the little bodies sitting next to her.

"You're fine? Roy didn't hurt you this time?" Her mom said no. "Mom, I've been so worried. They said it would work, that I didn't have…. You're really coming here? Now?"

"Yes." She heard her mom sob, and she cried too. The little boy hugged her hard, and she hugged him back. When he handed her a stuffed dog, she wasn't sure what to do with it, so he took it from her and used it to wipe her tears. Her dad came on the line while she was laughing at little George.

"That's what I needed to hear. Just you laughing made that sock in the jaw well worth it. Are you doing okay, honey? Your mom is blubbering a mile a minute." She nodded, then spoke.

"I'm fine now. So fine." She smiled, then remembered what he'd said. "Who hit you? They said you wouldn't be hurt. Tell me who hit you."

"Now, Jonny, it was necessary for that young man to make me fall and hit my head. It had to sound real if they were—"

"You hit your head too?" Jonny took a deep breath. "Dad, let me talk to Marc, please? I'd like to have a few words with him."

Marc came on the line and started talking before she had a chance to ask him. "I was supposed to make it look good. I think your dad actually enjoyed it. That is up until he hit his head. He wasn't supposed to grab the plates either, but he said it had better sound effects than him just falling like he was supposed to do, and Walker said the cut should heal pretty nicely. The bump looks a lot worse than it is, but again Walker said he'd be fine." He stopped talking, and she had to smile when he spoke again. "Jonny, are you going to hurt me when I get home?"

"You deserve it. What the hell were you thinking hitting a man, a human man like that?" She smiled when he started again. "I'm kidding. I'm so grateful that you all made it out that I can't…I don't know what to say."

"You don't have to say anything. We actually…Dylan and I have decided that we're never going to sell magazines door to door again. Women are…someone tried to seduce us. She came out of her kitchen naked." She laughed and sat down again holding the little animal while he told her what had happened with getting her parents out.

"You all really are fine?" He told her that they were. "I don't know how to thank you and your family for what you did for me. I feel so much better knowing that they're safe from him."

"It was my pleasure." She heard him say something to someone else, and then a door close. "We should be landing in about an hour. The pilot said that there is a good wind behind us."

"Khan said I couldn't come to meet you in case Roy is watching the house. Once my parents come through the gate here, he won't know that they're here either. He said that staying here will keep them safer." She leaned back in the chair when Corrine took little George for his bath. "I had a talk with your brother and your dad while you were gone. They said that you and I are connected and that when I leave, you'll be able to find me. Is that true?"

He was quiet for a few seconds. "Do you want to leave me, Jonny? Because I don't want you to. I need you in my life, and the thought of you even thinking about leaving is tearing me apart."

"I'm not cut out for being a domestic cat or human, Marc. I can barely boil water without having four pots involved. You saw what I ate all the time. It was cheap, sure, but it was all I trusted myself to cook."

"I can cook. Besides, we can hire someone for that part. It's the other fringe benefits I love about having you around." She asked him what kind of benefits. "Well, there's the fact that you can wash my back for me in the shower. A man can't have a too clean back. Then there's the little fact that you smell really good. Especially when you're wet for me. Do you have any idea how much I love that scent?"

"You make me wet just by talking to me in that low, rumbling voice. And when you touch my skin…Marc, this isn't a good idea. I'm going to need to take a cold shower if we don't stop this now." He growled and she felt her pussy soak.

"My cock is hard right now. And I can't wait to get home to take you. I don't even care if it's in a bed or in the hall. Slide your fingers into your pussy and tell me how wet you are, and I'll try not to come all over my hand when you do." She looked around the room to make sure she was alone before she slid her fingers over her soaking crotch. She moaned in the phone.

"I'm very wet. My jeans are wet all the way through." He growled at her to go to their bedroom they were using while they were at Khan's. She ran up the stairs and locked the door behind her. Telling him to hang on, she stripped down and got on the bed.

"Where are you?" She told him. "Christ, I wish I was there. Touch yourself for me, Jonny. Tell me how you feel."

"Wet. And hot. My fingers are coated with my juices, and my clit is hard." She brushed against it and moaned. "Marc, I'm going to come like this. Will you come with me?"

"Yes. I'm going to come just thinking about you playing with that beautiful pussy of yours." She heard him moan. "My balls are full and they're aching. When I get home I'm going to lean you over a chair and I'm going to fuck you hard from behind. Then when you're able to move again, I'm going to take you into the woods and let my cat take you. Would you like that? Him to fuck your cat hard out in the woods?"

She cried out her climax when she thought of him doing just that, his body pressing her down to the ground as he took her hard. When he roared out his own release, she came again, saying his name over and over as she pinched her clit. She lay there as both their breathing slowed back to normal.

"Christ, that was fantastic." She laughed at him. "I've never had phone sex before. I never dreamed it could be so…fulfilling."

"Neither did I. But I have to take a shower anyway. I'm a mess." He moaned again and she laughed. "You can't possibly think that it's sexy to be all sticky after sex."

"I find everything about you sexy, especially when you're all sticky after sex. I'd like it better if I was the one who got you all sticky, but I'll take care of that when I get home. I'm planning to make you extremely sated as well."

He told her again what had happened with her parents, but he didn't mention her dad's fall and the stitches again.

She was grateful for that; she didn't want to think about him being hurt. She told him about what his dad had said about her birth parents.

"You had to know that they couldn't be your real parents, right?" She told him that she'd figured it out when she'd shifted and they didn't know what to do. "I'm sure they didn't. You think it was the first time they realized that you were something different than them?"

"I do. Mom was completely freaked out, and Dad…well, you've met him. Nothing much fazes him, but my going from little girl not wanting to be told she couldn't go out with a much older boy to a panther snarling at him made him say a few curse words I'd never heard before, and pretty sure I've not heard since."

He laughed. "I'm thinking you're not much different now than you were then. Maybe a little more…vocal than before, but just as stubborn."

She stretched out on the bed as she thought of Roy. "He's going to be really mad when he finds that Mom and Dad are gone, won't he? He won't be able to use them against me again."

"No, he won't, and we're hoping he's mad. Angry people make ten times more mistakes than people who are calm and collected." She heard another voice. "The pilot just announced that we'll be landing in a few minutes. I'll see you in about an hour, okay?"

"I'll be here." She heard him speak again and closed her eyes. "Marc, if after this is over you want me to go away, I will, but I'll stay until this man is behind bars."

"I won't ever want you to leave me. Never, Jonny." He cleared his throat. "I've fallen in love with you."

She lay there for ten minutes, thinking about what he'd said. He loved her. How was that even possible when he knew so little about her? Getting up, she went to the shower and decided to take a bath, something she'd not been able to do in years. Filling the tub, she thought about him and what he'd done for her and with her. She was stepping into the tub when she realized something.

"I'm in love with him too."

CHAPTER 9

Roy walked around the house again. He couldn't believe that they'd left and no one had seen it happen. Well they had, but they didn't notice that they were leaving for good. He stepped over the body of one of the guards and moved to the basement again. Nothing. There wasn't a damned thing in the entire house that even looked like anyone lived there. Not one stick of furniture and not even a box of corn flakes. Everything was gone.

Harris came down the stairs just as Roy was going back up them. "Have you found out anything? I mean how the fuck did they get an entire house full of furniture and personal items out of here so quickly?"

"Don't know. But you should know that Anita is on her way here. She's spitting mad too." Like he needed that right now, Roy thought. "Something else. I found some tire marks in the backyard. Looks heavy when it drove off, probably loaded with the furniture."

No shit, he thought, and moved to the empty kitchen again and leaned against the counter. The older Thomas had had an apparent heart attack just two days ago. The men that had been stationed to watch the house had gone to get dinner before they'd called it in. Harris told them to go to the hospital and find out what they could on the couple and to call him back. It was nearly seven hours later before anyone did. And that conversation would be burned in his memory forever.

"We can't find them. We've been to five different hospitals and nobody seems to know nothing about nobody named Thomas being admitted. He and his missus ain't nowhere." Roy had listened to the entire conversation via speakerphone.

"You mean to tell me that an ambulance came to the house, took the couple away, and not one hospital has a record of it?" He didn't answer his question right away, but before Roy could tell him to fucking answer him, the idiot spoke.

"Well, you see…the ambulance that was here was called City Ambulance. There ain't no City Ambulance nowhere. We even checked with the local firehouse. He said he ain't never heard of it." The man gave a little laugh before he continued. "It might be one of those fly-by-night kinds. You know, here today and gone today."

Roy stepped out of his house, pulled his gun, and fired three times into the air. It was either do that or he would have shot the fucking phone. He had walked back into the house to tell Harris to stay at the house and wait for him. He'd be there in the morning.

And when they arrived at the house, it was to find it empty of every possession the couple had owned. Not only that, but someone had cleaned the place up and even swept the fucking floor. There were still marks on the carpet from it. He glared at the note again.

"You know that's what chaps my ass the most. The fucking bastards had left a note." He picked it up again, this time having to straighten it out after he'd crumpled it.

"Thank you for stopping by," the note read. "Sorry they're not here, but we gave the Thomases a better life, one that guaranteed that they would live a good deal longer. Fondly yours…."

"Who do you suppose left it?" Harris said. Roy glared at him. "I'm only asking because if we knew that, then we could find them, and then Jonny."

"No shit, you fucking genius. You think that, do you?" Roy walked away before he killed him too, mimicking the man. "*Because if we knew that, then we could find them, and then Jonny.*"

He had to find her. His clients were starting to get pissed about the deposit they'd given him and no panther. How the fuck was he supposed to run a business when his star attraction was nowhere to be found? Damn it, all she had to do was hang around their house for a few days, steal a few things that they wouldn't even miss, and then go someplace else. What the fuck was her problem? And now that he'd "killed" her friend, and someone had taken her parents, he had nothing to hold over her.

"Boss, do you want me to have one of the wolves have a look around? They might not be able to find the truck, but they might be able to find out who helped them." Roy nodded at Harris.

The wolves were stupid anyway. He figured that they'd be lucky they could find their own ass, much less find a couple who, for all intents and purposes, had been cleaned from this house completely. He watched as they moved past him into the house.

The first one came out almost immediately, the other three less than a minute behind. He watched them roll in the grass for several minutes before they moved as far from the house as they could get. Roy looked at Harris when he stepped out as well.

"What the fuck is that about?"

Harris shrugged. "Well, ask them. Something either scared the shit out of them or they got a whiff of something."

"Can't. Not for an hour at least. They can't shift back. Wolves have to stay as they are for at least an hour." Roy asked him if he was fucking kidding. "Nope. It's what makes them nearly unreliable as a house pet. Once they get into the house and then report back as a human, they have to stay that way, as a human for an hour. People tend to miss them when they can't find them after that long."

Roy sat down on the deck and put his head on his hands. This was a fucking nightmare. He had shifters, about a dozen of them, that couldn't be a panther for some dumb fucking reason, wolves that had to be a wolf for an hour, and a panther that fucking wasn't cooperating. And now this house. He looked over the yard and started to laugh when he noticed that there wasn't even a bit of lawn furniture. He looked up when Anita walked out to where he was.

"Where the hell is the furniture?" Roy started laughing. Tears were streaming down his face, and every time he looked at the wolves at the back of the property with their tails between their legs, he would laugh more. Finally, when he thought he could control himself, he told her what had happened. She wasn't any happier about it than he was.

~~~

Marc was in his office looking over the file he'd been looking at for the past ten minutes without seeing it when someone knocked. He looked up to see Dylan and Jack
~~~

walk in. Jack had a laptop in her hand, and Dylan wore a grin.

"What the hell is up with you two? And I thought you weren't going to be back here for a few more weeks." Jack nodded and came around to his side of the desk.

"I've been looking up some information that Jacob gave me. It's about Jonny." She laughed when another knock sounded at his door. "That would be her now."

Marc smiled at Jonny as she walked in. She blushed when he wiggled his brows at her, and he nearly burst out laughing when Dylan asked her to have a seat. She moved as far from him as she could.

"What's the matter, honey, don't you trust me?" She snorted at Dylan. "Ah, that's no way to treat the man who saved your family's treasures."

"Did he tell you what he did?" Jonny said. He shook his head at her and looked at his brother. "He had someone go into my parents' home and pack everything up. Every piece of furniture they had and their safe in the basement. It was delivered today and put into storage for them. He told me he had the place cleaned too. And fucking marked."

Dylan laughed as he tried to defend himself. "I knew that they'd try to find out who helped them, and I didn't know how much of Marc and I we'd left behind. Would you have felt better if they could have figured out that a different panther had helped them escape?"

Marc started to tell his brother not to piss Jonny off, that she had a short fuse, but decided he was on his own. He watched them out of the corner of his eye while Jack pulled up something from a thumb drive.

"You don't think that someone is going to tell them who did it?" Jonny demanded. Dylan shook his head. "And why the fuck is that?"

"Because their neighbors helped me move everything out." Jonny's mouth closed and she looked at him before turning back to Dylan as he continued. "I had gone over to their house as soon as Marc left. I, as you know, was going back to get my wife, but decided to help your parents out. I liked them."

"I do too. But that doesn't negate the fact that you might have gotten caught there. How do you think my mom and dad would have felt if you'd gotten hurt moving their stuff out if Roy caught you there?"

"I told the two goons to not say anything about the move until we were finished. Besides, they were very helpful in carrying the larger pieces. And when the neighbors saw what was going on, they helped too. When I couldn't get a couple of the larger pieces on the truck, Mr. Sanders let me store it in his garage. And Mrs. Granger was nice enough to take all the food to the local pantry. She even cleaned the place up for us. After everyone was gone, I went back in and…." He grinned at him. "I made sure that nothing but another panther would be able to enter the place and try to scent us out. They'll be useless as a hunter as soon as they get a whiff of the calling card I left behind."

"I don't understand," Jonny said, and looked at him as he shook his head. "You aren't going to tell me?"

"I don't think you want to know. Suffice it to say that a panther's urine is very toxic to other animals. That's why it's so hard to track us even in the wild."

"You pissed in the house?" She stood up and looked down at Dylan. "You pissed in my parents' house?" He nodded.

Jonny sat down. She looked pole axed, but Marc didn't blame her. She knew so little about what she was and what she could do that he wanted to take her aside and tell her everything. His mom had given her a book about panther legend, but she'd barely scratched the surface since this had been going on.

"I found something." Marc looked up at Jack, completely forgetting that she had said she had something to tell him. "I'm not going to tell you where I got this information, and I won't share it with just anyone, but you two, I trust you."

Marc thanked her and looked at the charts on her computer. "What is it I'm looking at? And why do I care?"

"You should care because it's a list of every panther ever born. And will be born." He looked at her sharply. "You can't ask. But I can tell you what Dylan and I have found out about our Jonny here."

"Me? But your dad, he told me who my biological parents are. He said my father is dead and about my mother, he had no idea. And no, before you ask, I haven't asked Mom and Dad how they managed to end up with me."

"They ended up with you because someone left you on their doorstep, quite literally." While Jack pointed to the entry, Jonny came to sit on his lap. "According to this entry, you were left by someone by the name of 'Bob.' There are no other references to him other than that. But you should know that both your parents are alive. Your mom is in a zoo and is shackled so she can't shift, and your father…."

"My father what?" Jack sat down and glanced at Dylan, who nodded at her to continue. Marc pulled Jonny closer to him, knowing that she was going to be upset by whatever Jack told her.

"Your father is her keeper. He works at the zoo and specializes in panthers. Your mother is one of his animals. The rest of the information says that he keeps her like that so that she can't harm anyone again. She was sentenced to where she is by the council after the trial. The band on her ankle is magical, but no one but your father can see it. She's bound there until she dies. And when she does, your father has asked to die with her. It's the pact they made with the council."

"There's more, isn't there?" Jonny sat up and looked at Jack and Dylan. "I don't know how you got this information, and I don't really care, but I want to know the rest."

Dylan cleared his throat. "Your mother was pregnant with you when she decided that she would rob a bank. The bank had been hit the week before and your mother decided that it would be a good time to hit it again. She was heard to say that no one would think that it would be hit so soon and they'd be more relaxed. She was wrong. As soon as they entered, it went from bad to worse in seconds. They killed three people, including the bank manager and a child. They never left the building with any money."

"You said 'they.' Who was with her? I'm assuming it wasn't my father." Dylan shook his head. "Then who, damn it. Stop fucking beating around the bush and tell me."

"It was Anita Kidd's older brother, Samuel Kidd. According to witnesses, he knew that the game was over. He was reported begging her to stop, and when she didn't, he started letting the hostages go without her knowing. When she eventually found out, she shot him in the head and killed him."

"She sold me out to Roy because my mother had her brother killed." Marc could feel her shock and pulled her to him again, but she pulled away and started pacing the room. "Why didn't they kill her, my mother, I mean? Because of me, right?"

"Yes, that and the fact that they wanted her to suffer. She hated children, and the council decided that her best course of punishment was to have her around them all the time. Your father stayed with her because she is his mate. He can't leave her no matter what she tried to do to you."

"She tried to kill me?" Jack nodded at Jonny's question. "I have a scar in my shoulder. I often wanted to ask about it, but whenever Mom saw it, she would turn away, like it hurt her or something knowing that it was there. How did she do it?"

"It doesn't say. It only says that you have a scar on your left shoulder and that it is unknown as to how you received it." Jack got up and walked to her. "I'm sorry, Jonny. I truly am. But I knew that you'd want to know what you're up against."

Jonny nodded, and a few minutes later Jack and Dylan left. Dylan told him to contact him if she had any questions, and he promised him he would. Jonny stood by the window and stared out it. He wasn't sure what to do to help her with this.

"Your brother asked me to pledge myself to him. I told him I'd talk to you. I'm not really sure what it means, but he said that basically I tell him that he can pretty much ruin my night when he can contact me at a whim."

That sounded like something that Khan would say. "You would tell him that he is your leader and that you would abide by any rules he sets forth."

She snorted. "Like that's going to happen. Do you think my father wanted to see me?"

He was getting used to her swift change of subject and was able to answer her. "I don't know, but if you want we can go and see them both. Or just your father. Jack said she'd give you the name of the zoo if you decided that is something you'd want to do."

She shook her head. "I'm not ready for a family reunion just yet. Besides, she might still be a little pissed at me because I didn't die when she tried to hurt me. Do you think Roy knows what's going on?"

"It's hard to say. You told me that the day you left that Anita was in his bedroom. Had you ever seen them in the room together before?"

"No. In fact, that was the first time I'd been in that part of the house before. I was just coming down the windows when I heard her talking." She turned to him. "Now that I think on it, I got out fairly easy. Do you think they planned it that way?"

"I doubt they expected you to actually get away. They probably figured that you'd get that far and then you'd walk in on the *murder*. I'm pretty sure you were early and heard them reading from a script like you thought. They were more than likely still practicing when you over heard them. Otherwise, they would have taken more care not to have Anita laugh when you left."

"They didn't find me until several hours later. I know that because I was on foot and they were in cars. I had shifted, of course, to get that far, but it was still a long way to go and I got lost twice." Marc nodded. "She'd become my friend to set me up."

"I'm afraid so, love." She stood there for several more minutes before he stood up to stand behind her. She leaned back against his body when he wrapped his arms around her waist.

"I'm sorry." He asked her for what. "All this. You couldn't have known that having me for a mate would be so complicated. I'm betting you're regretting this about now."

"Never. I told you before that I was falling in love with you, but I'm not anymore." She turned in his arms and looked at him. "I've fallen in love with you. I do too. I love you with all my heart."

Marc held her until his phone rang and let her go, regrettably, to answer it. He picked it up and smiled at his mom. He glanced at Jonny before he answered her.

"Yes, we'll be home for dinner tonight. And I'll ask her about the other. Or he can when we get there." He hung up and walked back over to her. "My mom is expecting us for dinner, and little George wants to know if you'll read him a story again."

"He's a cute kid. Smart too. Do you want kids someday?" Smiling, he pulled her into his arms for a long, sensual kiss before answering her.

"Why, Miss Jonny, are you propositioning me? If you are, then yes, I want kids. If not…." He grinned. "If not, then I will proposition you and have a baby with you anyway."

CHAPTER 10

They drove back to Marc's house after dinner. Khan's house was getting really full, and when Marc suggested they go back there, she had agreed. Besides, she wanted to sleep in the big bed he had. Plus, he had promised her a run, and she felt as if she needed it now more than ever.

"Mom said she'd set us up with housekeepers to interview within a few days. I hope you don't mind that I asked her to help." She shook her head. What did she know about interviewing for a housekeeper?

"She would know more about what you need than I do, I guess." She wandered around the living room, then the kitchen. She knew that he followed her, but she really didn't care. What she needed was some fresh air and alone time.

"I'm going out." She opened the door and was standing on the deck when he came out. "I want to be alone. I have things to think about and I…I'll be back."

"No." She turned to look at him. "No, you can't go off and think on your own. I want to talk about whatever it is that's bothering you."

Where to start? She looked out in the woods that seemed to be in the backyard of all their homes. All their big-assed homes. Their furniture was really nice, some of it really old but in beautiful shape. And they had nannies and maids, things she didn't understand or know what to do with. And they were violent at times, more so than she'd ever seen when it came to their families.

"My parents are a little overwhelmed by all of you. Mom said she felt like she was living in a castle staying with Khan and Monica. I told her she didn't have to curtsy when they came in the room." It was supposed to be a joke, but she knew even to herself it sounded lame. "My dad isn't used to not going to work either. He's worried he'll lose his job."

"I have a couple of houses they can live in if they want after this is over. Or they can go back to their home too, when this is over. You have to know that they're safer here with all of us." She nodded. "What else is wrong, Jonny?"

"You saw where I grew up. You had to notice that you're way above me in the blue blood scale. I'm not ashamed at my home, but it's nothing like this. My parents have to work to make ends meet. I do too. You sort of come and go as you please because there are others to help you out. I've never…my family and I have never had that. We've only ever had each other."

When he started to step toward her, she stepped off the deck. He moved to the railing around them and leaned into it as he watched her. She was trying to tell him what she wanted him to understand, but she felt she wasn't telling it right.

"I don't know how to be one of you guys." He laughed. "I'm trying to tell you that I don't know how you expect this to work out. Your parents are the nicest people I've met and have treated me really well, but I'm just a panther they're trying to help out, I think. Your brothers are amazing and rich and seem to like me okay. But I don't know how to act around them."

"You don't need to *act* at all, Jonny. Just be yourself. When you're standoffish to them they think you don't like them." She looked at him and started to deny what he said, but he cut her off. "You do. Even at dinner tonight you sat next to me and hardly said a word. Sebastian tried to get to know you, but you only gave him one-syllable answers until he just gave up. He asked me if you hated him."

"I'm afraid for them to touch me." She flushed when she realized how loudly she'd said that. "I don't want you to kill any of them because they touched me. Your dad said that a male could and would kill to protect what he has claimed. He was telling me a story about this man he'd seen torn apart because he had the nerve to touch another man's female."

"He raped her, not touched her." She looked at Marc. "And I'm going to kill my father the next time I see him."

"No. Don't do that. He's really old, but he's nice. I think he was trying to tell me not to go around hugging people. He said it would make you want to kill, and then you'd mark me again."

Marc laughed. "Yes, he's going to die a slow and painful death. He was kidding you, love. He's the most lovable, ornery man I know. And he doesn't know when to quit. I won't kill any of my brothers because they touched you. So long as they know that there is touching and there is hurting. And when you get back to me, I'm going to mark you again. Everywhere I can."

He moved toward her, and she stood still on the step. She wanted him to touch her, to mark her, but she wasn't sure how to tell him that. When he pulled her into his arms, she went to him willingly and laid her head on his chest.

"I can smell Monica on you. And your mom. I don't feel the least bit like going out and killing them." He chuckled. "You know, I think I'd like to handle your dad. I think there are some ground rules he and I are going to put down, and I'm going to make him pay for making me a nervous wreck all night."

"Good. I'll play along. Khan too. I'm betting any of them will be willing to help you out." He lifted her chin. "You need to understand something. Everything I have is yours. Everything, Jonny. This house, the money, the buildings and property? All if it belongs to you as much as it does me. And as for your parents? They are as welcome into our family as you are. If they want, we'll put them into a castle if we can find one and hire all the people they want to wait on them."

"I doubt they'd want that. My mom has been a housewife all her life. And dad has been a beat cop longer than I can remember. He is terrified of losing his pension as well as his seniority. The house isn't even paid off."

He was quiet for several minutes, and she realized how incredibly quiet it was around them. Her parents' house was on a busy, rundown street that had things going on all the time. And not in the good neighbor sort of way, either. There were drug deals going down daily and police cars making runs down their street nightly. She looked up at him when he started to speak.

"I was going to say that I'd take care of that for you, but I realize that you'd be pissed at me again. And since I have plans for that luscious body of yours later, I have decided to be man enough to ask for your help in helping them." He grinned. "How would you like to make it so that your parents aren't worried so much?"

"What do you mean?" She followed him to the chair and sat in his lap when he patted it. She watched him as he seemed to be working something out in his mind. When he smiled at her, she felt like the sun had warmed her.

"I have money and you have money as well. A great deal of it. Not endless, mind you, but close. I've invested well, and when Walker married Caitlynne, she gave each of us a substantial amount of money as well. She paid off all our debts, and if our houses were paid for, she gave us enough to purchase another. Her money is pretty much endless." She started to ask him what this had to do with her parents when he kissed her quiet. "Now, as I said, we have a few houses that we rent out. They are in good neighborhoods and within a few miles of us. I think, as a couple, you and I should discuss having your parents, if they want to, move into one of them as a gift to us for our wedding."

"I didn't know we were getting married." He laughed and asked her to stand up for a second. "No, I like it right here for now. You will explain what you mean by the wedding comment."

"I can't if you're sitting on my lap." She stood up and he turned her and sat her in the chair. "I meant to do this yesterday, but we were sort of busy with other things."

He reached into his pocket and pulled out a tiny little box. She stood up quickly, only to be pressed back down into the chair. When Marc knelt down on one knee, she tried to stand again.

"This will work much better if you don't keep acting like a jack-in-the-box and let me propose to you." He slipped the ring on her finger to the first knuckle and held his hand across her lap at the same time. "Damn but you're stubborn, aren't you? Jonny Thomas, I would very much like for you to become my wife. As soon as possible. Tomorrow, if I can arrange it."

"Marry you?" He nodded and pushed the ring all the way onto her finger. "You can't possibly think that…I thought we were going to discuss our staying together after this thing with Roy was over?"

"Well, I don't really think that's going to be necessary, do you? I love you, and I'm reasonably sure you love me as well." She just stared at the ring. "You're supposed to say 'why, yes, Marc, I love you very much,' not stare at the ring like you've never seen one before."

"I haven't. Not on my hand anyway. This is what you want?" Marc shook his head. "You've already changed your mind?"

"No, this is what *we* want. You do, don't you, Jonny? You want to be my wife?" He kissed her hand and held it to his cheek. "You wouldn't want to break my poor little heart would you?"

"What if we—?" He cut her off with a kiss. She melted into him as he stood and pulled her to her feet as well. When he lifted his head, she blinked several times, trying to bring things back into focus.

"We could 'what if' this to death and we'd never be married. We could think of all sorts of reasons why we shouldn't do this and not be together. Or we could just skip all that in favor of saying yes and worry about everything else as it comes." He kissed her again. "I love you. I want to be with you. I want to have babies with you. I especially want to work on having those babies with you."

She laughed. "Why yes, Marc, I love you very much and would love to spend the rest of my life giving you a hard time and making you want to pull your hair out."

He hugged her tightly. “Close enough. But I think I’ll have to teach you to be romantic. You’re a little on the weird side.”

~~~

Roy watched the video again. He didn’t see what had Harris all in a tizzy, but he was willing, for now, to give him the benefit of the doubt. He peered closer to the computer when he indicated that it was coming up. Then he saw her.

“Christ.” Harris nodded as Roy backed the DVD up to watch it again. She was at a cash register in the same fucking town as they were right now. They had given up looking there after she’d run, thinking that she would have been long gone, and as far from them as she could get. And here she was hiding under their fucking noses.

“I told you I’d find her. According to the manager of the store, she wasn’t a regular but he remembered her. She said that she owed him some extra money on account of her getting home and realizing that she’d not paid for something, a coat or some shit. He said he remembered her ‘cause of that. And she was a beauty.”

Roy nodded, trying to think what to do now. The shifter that they’d bought from Kidd had turned out to be a dud. Who knew that in order to shift to a panther you needed permission from the local family? He’d had to look up what the fuck he’d been talking about and found that a pack of panthers was called that. A family. What a lame-assed name for a bunch of big fucking predators like cats. He personally would have called them a pack, sounded so much better than a family.

“Have we got someone watching this store front?” Harris nodded. “It’s doubtful that she’ll return, but it’s
~~~

good to know that she's close. Stupid bitch will be mine before too much longer."

"There are like six empty buildings around that store. All owned by the same company. Bowen something…I don't remember. But I asked around and none of the other store owners have seen her. I was gonna go and see that Bowen guy tomorrow. He's got some sort of insurance place about a block from the Vintage place."

"Good. That's good. And when you get back, swing by the office and tell me what you found." Harris nodded and left. Anita came through the door as he was leaving and Roy found himself putting his hand on his gun.

"You find her yet?" He told her what Harris had just relayed to him. "She's as good as dead, you know that, right? As soon as this fucking thing with pets is fulfilled, I'm going to take her out into the woods and blow her fucking brains out."

"We could make a million off just her if we keep her around. I'm not kidding, Anita, I've got them lined up out the fucking door wanting a female panther roaming around their yards. We could practically own this business." She shook her head. "Then give me a year with her. After that we should have enough money put away that we can go wherever we want."

"I can go wherever I want now. Daddy would send me just to get rid of me." She had that right. Her dad had called him just last night asking if she was in danger. When he'd told the man he was keeping his daughter safe, he'd told him not to bother, he wouldn't.

"She's an evil psychopath that should have been locked up years ago. Not only that, but she spends more money on drugs than ten men I have selling it for me. I've had it with her. She's not been right since her brother and mother passed." The older man had broken down after that. "Anita is my only living child and I can't stand to be in the same room with her any more than it takes for me to hand her some cash. What kind of father thinks that about his own child?"

"I don't know, sir." And Roy hadn't. He'd been dealing with her for less than five years and she seemed to get worse all the time. When she'd found out that his panther was Jonny Thomas, she'd gone over the edge. It had taken him nearly a week to get his office back to rights.

"You mark my words, Dawson, if you don't get rid of her—and I mean get rid of her—she will bring you down with her. She's nothing but trouble. And she creates it when she can't get anyone else to."

And now she sat in Roy's office, bitching about how much she wanted Jonny killed. He had always wanted to ask her what she'd done to her, but had been afraid of her rage. So he'd looked it up.

There hadn't been anything or, it seemed, any contact between her and Thomas until he found the article about Anita's brother, Samuel, being killed. After reading the article twice, he finally saw what he'd thought was a connection. There had been mention, only slightly, that a panther had been seen within the bank he and a woman named Deb Anderson had been in the process of robbing when the young man Samuel had been killed by his partner. After paying out an ungodly amount of money to have records searched, he found that Deb had been sent to prison and that she had a child. That was all there was, and no matter how much he paid, there had never been any mention of her again. But he had found a picture of Anderson and was amazed at how much the woman looked like his Jonny Thomas.

"Are you even listening to a fucking word I'm saying?" He looked up at her, trying to remember what she'd said. "I fucking don't believe you. I said we should simply put out a hit on her. Daddy does it all the time and it usually takes care of the problem in no time."

"I need her to fulfill my contracts. If she's dead, I'm going to have to pay back every penny to those waiting for her, and that's a great deal of money. Money that mostly went up your nose." He snapped his mouth closed when he realized that he'd spoken out loud. "I didn't mean that. But I'm nervous about this falling through."

"You think I like snorting coke? You think I like being high all the fucking time?" He was pretty sure she did but didn't say anything. But he did put his finger on the trigger when she stood up to come around to his side of the desk.

"You could get help." She snorted at him. "Your father said he'd pay for it, you said. You told me that he promised to give you a million dollars if you completed the program and remained sober and clean for a year. That's a lot of money, Anita."

"Yes it is, but it's not even a drop in the bucket to what he's really worth. I just figure that he'll die soon enough and I'll get all of it without having to be a goody two-shoes." She staggered to his liquor cabinet and poured herself about three cups of bourbon into a glass. "I know what he does for a living and I know how much he's worth too. Billions upon billions, and it'll all be mine someday."

Heaven help us was Roy's only thought. She moved to the chair again and nearly tipped it over trying to sit. He didn't get up to help her…he was afraid to get too close to her. She tended to lash out when she didn't want help and cry when you gave it to her. She was a fucking wreck.

"I'm going to make her pay for what she did to me. That fucking kid shouldn't have a life after her mother killed my only friend." She started crying, and Roy sat very still. She was like a time bomb and he wasn't going to be hit with any flying pieces when she exploded.

"You should just go to bed, Anita. Take a long nap, and when you wake, you'll feel much differently." She shook her head. "Please, Anita, I need this girl. She's going to make me a very wealthy man."

"I don't care about you and your damned money. I only agreed to help you so that I could get close to her so I could kill her. And I'm going to kill her too. Dead." She stood, reached her hand into her pocket, and pulled out a gun, and his entire body went on alert. "With this gun right here. This is the one her cunt of a mom killed my brother with, and then she just stepped over him like he was nothing. Nothing. Oh yeah, she's dead all right. Dead. Dead. Dead."

She moved out of the room, still waving her gun. When he heard her go up the stairs, he let out his breath. Christ, she was going to hurt him if he didn't do something about her soon. And he would have to make it permanent.

CHAPTER 11

There was something incredibly sexy about waking next to a naked woman. He supposed that he being naked as well helped. Rolling over so that he spooned in behind her, Marc licked along her shoulder. Christ, he could get used to his.

"You're supposed to sleep late. Isn't that what you said when we went to bed?" She looked over her shoulder and smiled at him. "It's not late yet. It's only five in the morning."

"You woke me. It's entirely your fault I'm awake." He rocked into her ass and heard her moan. "See? That's why. You're just way too sexy to let lay there all warm and cozy."

She rolled to her belly, and he over her. Sitting up and straddling her thighs, he ran his finger up her spine and back down. She responded by moaning his name, and he leaned down and kissed her.

"How about a massage?" She moaned again and he rubbed his hands up her ribs and down her back. "You're very beautiful even like this."

Moving up over her ass so he could reach her shoulders, he began digging his fingers into her muscles. She wasn't tense, but she was firm, her body tone, as well, defined. Bringing her arms down, he rubbed her bicep, digging his fingers deep into the muscle and then down to her forearm and wrist. He took her fingers and rotated them, pushing his thumbs deep and hard. Then he repeated the same process on her other side.

Her back was next. Down her spine and up he worked her scapula, his thumbs digging again until she was putty. Her ribs beckoned him, and he leaned down and nipped at her tender flesh. Moving down to her thighs, he ran his hand over her lovely ass.

His cock ached to be inside of her as he pulled and dug at her muscles. He could smell her arousal so strongly that he could swear he could taste it on his tongue. Moving down her body was becoming a painful experiment, but he was enjoying himself. Each time she moaned, said his name on a soft sigh, he felt his love for her strengthen and grow.

Sliding off her, he lifted her leg. As soon as he did, he nearly fell over her and took her. Her scent was calling to him, and he had to concentrate hard on what he was doing. He thought talking would help.

"I want to run with you again. Last night was too short." That wasn't helping. It had been short because he'd lost her twice in the woods. She was good at hiding out.

"You want to run with me now?" He stopped massaging her foot and looked up at her as she stared over her shoulder. "The thought of you taking me, chasing me, has me…please?"

All he could manage was "go." He sat there for ten seconds after she got up before he could move off the bed to follow her. When he entered the kitchen, the door was open to the outside and he just caught a glimpse of her as her cat darted toward the woods.

He leapt from the deck and shifted at the same time. His body seemed to scream out its joy at being free. His cat snarled and kept running after his mate. Marc smiled, thinking there was not going to be anything short about this run.

He could smell her at every turn. She was moving quickly and leaving him a trail that screamed for him to find her. He spotted her once as she moved between trees, and then again when she jumped at him, knocking him to the ground and rolling him over. She was gone again before he could get up. He didn't just want her now, he had to have her.

He hunkered down and waited. Her scent was all around him and he knew now that the only way to catch her was to outsmart her. He had a thought that outsmarting her was going to be just as hard, but decided never to tell her that. She might just outsmart him again.

He heard her before he saw her. She was barely making a sound, and he probably wouldn't have heard her at all if it hadn't been for him being so close. She moved by him slowly, her paws barely touching the ground. When she moved past him, he nearly forgot what he was doing, he'd been so caught up in her beauty.

When she was only a foot away, he stood and jumped at the same time. He brought her down quickly but had to scramble to hold her. As soon as he was over her, she reared up and snarled. Marc bit her shoulder hard to hold her down. He put his paw on her back and held her there while he positioned himself behind her. She fought harder until he had to bite her harder.

Christ, if I last longer than a second inside of you I'll be amazed. Moving closer, he pressed her harder into the ground while he mounted her. She was so wet that he slid in and moaned. His cock filled her so tightly that it took him several seconds to realize that she was a virgin like this. And that she was biting his forearm.

Lifting his head from her shoulder, he licked the wound and felt her let go of his arm. He moved in and out of her slowly and let her get used to him. His cat snarled, but for the most part, Marc wasn't an animal. Laughing to himself, he knew that with this woman he always would be.

When her ass came up to meet his strokes, he moved quicker and deeper. When he felt his balls tighten, ready to fill her, he bit her again. This time she didn't bite back, but he did feel her shift beneath him, her body milking him as she came. Marc threw back his head and roared out his own release.

Lying over her, he panted hard. He wanted more, he needed more, and shifted. His cock jerked and lengthen at the sight of her lying there, his mate. Ordering her to shift, she was human in seconds, her body still the way he'd taken her. Moving up behind her again, he slammed into her hard, gripping her hips and bringing her back to him with each pound into her. She moved up to her hands, her breasts swinging freely. He watched them, mesmerized how her nipples strained and her areolas darkened.

"Marc, please. I need you. Please." When she stretched up and wrapped her arms around his neck, he rolled back on his heels. Running his hands up her ribs, he cupped her breasts and tweaked at her hard peaks. He could bite her like this, sink his teeth into her and mark her again and again, but she was begging him for release and he wanted her to come with him.

"Lay down, baby. Let me make love to you." She moaned and moved off him. He looked down at his cock and fisted it as she lay there looking up at him. He wanted to come on her, he wanted to spew his cum all over her and rub it into her skin.

Her hands moved down from above her head and she filled them with her breasts. Marc moved closer to her, his thighs touching hers as he sat on his heels between her legs. He tightened around his shaft and slowly moved up and down it as he watched her.

"Touch yourself for me. I want to see you touch yourself like I imagined you doing while I was on the phone with you." Her hands moved down over her hips and brushed over her skin just above her neatly trimmed pussy. "That's it, baby. Bring yourself to peak so I can come all over you."

She bent her knees and opened her legs for him. He would remember this for the rest of his life, the sight of her exposed for him, like a feast that only he could enjoy. Watching had become both a pleasure and a painful experience. He wanted to be inside of her almost as much as he wanted to see his cum staining her skin.

When she slid her fingers into her nether lips, his cock began to seep. She danced first one, then another inside of her, teasing him with what she was doing. As soon as her free hand came down to join the first, she spread her lips wide and he nearly strangled his cock when he watched her finger her clit.

Her body rolled, her moans were louder, her keening less coherent. The faster her fingers moved and slipped inside of her the harder he pulled on his cock. When she stiffened, he did as well, his balls so tight to his body that he held them as they filled. When she screamed out his name and her body bowed up and her thigh touched his balls, Marc felt his climax run the length of his cock and out onto her.

He watched as his cum hit her nipple, her chin, and her belly. Great streams of it sprayed over her arms and her breasts. She ran her hand over it, rubbing it over her as she came again and again, her entire being taut with the strength of her release. Even as he continued to come he lifted her and buried his cock inside of her, taking her hard, filling her with yet another climax from his body. She wrapped her legs around him, pulled him down, and took his mouth. He could taste himself there; his cum was on her tongue, and he devoured her more just to taste them together. Fucking her through another release, he slowed, his body spent. Dropping down and rolling over to his back, he pulled her over him and closed his eyes. He couldn't have moved right now even if an entire platoon of soldiers came tromping by them.

When she sighed, he hugged her to him but didn't move to get up. Feeling his body come back to itself slowly, he was so relaxed that he knew that if he didn't get up now he might never. It was his last thought as sleep claimed him.

~~~

Jonny moved and her body screamed at her. Opening one eye, she realized that they were still in the woods and they were both naked, without any clothes to put on to go back to the house. She stretched over him and grinned as he opened his one eye. When he opened the other, she laughed.

"You don't wake very easily, do you?" She laughed harder when he growled. "We need to get going. Do you have any idea what time it might be?"
~~~

Marc shook his head and closed his eyes. "I don't really care either. As far as I'm concerned, if we spent the next hundred years out here doing what we'd did earlier, I'd die a happy man."

"Yes, and that won't be long because we'd starve to death first." She put her hand on her belly when it growled. "My belly thinks my throat has been cut. I'm going back to the house and having some cereal. Do you have any in that fancy kitchen of yours?"

"No fucking way. Cereal? Gross. Let me lie here for a few more minutes and I'll go inside and make you my famous pancakes and sausage links." She slapped his chest. "You are seriously violent in the morning, aren't you?"

"I don't want pancakes. I hate them." She nearly laughed when he sat up and looked at her, a shocked expression on his face. "All they are is soggy bread with liquid sugar all over them. Now that's gross. I want waffles. Thick ones too. Can you make that with all that equipment in your kitchen?"

"There is nothing wrong with my equipment, I'll have you know." He stood up and looked down at her. "What are you going to do, wait for me to bring it to you on a silver platter? Not going to happen. And if I cook, you have to clean up. Share and share alike, I think. Come on."

They walked hand and hand to the house. It didn't bother her as much as she thought it would to be naked and doing this. She had never been so happy in her life. She realized that they'd left the doors opened, and worried that someone or something had gotten in while they were gone.

"Smell the room. Do you smell anyone else?" She did as he asked as he handed her one of his shirts from the clean clothes on the washer. She pulled it over her head and brought the sleeve to her nose.

"I can smell you on this shirt and in this room but…nothing." He nodded as he pulled on the bottoms to the shirt she had on. "You wear pajamas?"

"Only when someone comes over to stay the night. About two weeks ago I had an all-nighter with my team and Dennis stayed here rather than drive all the way back. We were working on a case."

The phone rang as he was pulling out things from the refrigerator. He asked her to answer it. She tried to get out of it, but he insisted she'd have to sooner or later, and now was as good as time as any.

"Hello, my dear. It's George…the older one, not the baby. Though I'm thinking that he'll be answering the phone on his own soon enough. It's those Bowen genes, you see. They make for a much smarter panther than most." He laughed, as did she. "I don't suppose Marc is lying next to you, is he? I need to speak to him."

"We're in the kitchen, not the bed." She felt she owed him for his teasing her. "Actually, we didn't even use the bed last night. We've decided to have sex on every piece of furniture that is in here and out. And surfaces too. No wall too thin for us. Of course, we may need to replace the coffee table. Not as strong as it looked, I'm afraid. How long do you suppose it will take us?"

She glanced at Marc, who was holding his hand over his mouth and laughing so hard that he was bent over from it. His dad was sputtering on the phone so badly that she was sure he was soaking the sucker. She handed the phone to Marc when he could breathe normally again and sat on the counter to listen.

"She said…. Oh my, she is…Marc, I think…." Poor George seemed to be at a loss for words. "I think I will call you back. Whatever I had to say is…I just can't remember."

She laughed with Marc as he put the phone back on the charger. "I think you just got my dad the best he's ever been gotten. I've never heard him so dumbfounded in my life. I loved it. I love you."

"I love you too." He stilled and looked at her. "I do. You make it hard sometimes, but I think I've loved you all my life. Well, maybe wanted to love you all my life."

He pulled her off the counter and handed her a bowl. "Mix until I tell you to stop. It's time you learned to cook something besides noodles in a plastic bag."

"I can cook. I just choose not to." She glared at him when he swatted her ass. "I'll learn to cook just so I can know which poisons to mix with your food if you hit me like that again."

He laughed and went to the phone when it rang. He picked it up smiling, but after speaking to someone on the other end, his entire body language changed. She put down the bowl when he motioned her closer. He put his finger over his lips and put the phone on speaker.

"What did you say she looked like again? I'm not really very sure, and you can understand that I don't want anyone to get into trouble if I don't have the right information." He wrote a large question mark on the blackboard next to the phone as he asked the caller to repeat himself.

"Oh yeah, sure. Understand that completely. She's tall and sort of on the thin side. Not too skinny, just like one of those pretty fillies that you see on that channel that has animals. Dark hair and sort of black blue eyes. Not bruised, mind you, but the color. She sort of has this…well I don't want to say she's a bitch, but she can be mouthy when it suits her."

Jonny grabbed the table and shook her head. They'd found her. When she tried to back away, Marc grabbed her and pulled her to him. His whisper in her ear was low and urgent. She nodded when he handed her the chalk. He'd asked her who it was, and told her that he wasn't there. He promised her she was safe. She wanted to scream at him that she wasn't worried about her but only his safety, and that of his family. Trembling, she went to the chalkboard.

"Harris Manning, aka, henchman." He nodded and pulled her back into his arms. She tried not to listen to Harris talk to Marc, but she was too close to the phone not to hear him.

"She's been out for near a month now. Don't know what her family is gonna do when they find we misplaced her again. I'm guessing the doc here is gonna make her take something to keep her a little less a flight risk, if you know what I mean."

Marc laughed when Harris did. "Yes, I believe I do. But the person you described doesn't ring a bell. I mean, if you give me your number I could call you if I hear or see anything."

"Nah. I can call you. I might not have any service. You give me your number and I'll call you in a couple of days and we can see if you remember anything." Marc smiled at her when she heard the small beep.

"The service you called can get in touch with me. I'm in and out of the office so much that I really don't have a number. Every call goes right through them." She heard Harris say something about that being sad, but Marc continued. "You call me back on Wednesday. This is

Sunday, so four days might be enough for me to see what I can find out for you. That okay?"

"Yeah, I suppose. Really is a shame you don't have a number I can call you back on. Not even a cell phone number?" Marc told him no. "Okay then. I'll call you back on Wednesday. Thank you kindly."

She watched him as he put the phone on the charger again and pull out his cell phone. While it rang he looked at her with the biggest grin on his face. She smiled back, just happy to see it.

"I'm calling Reed and Sebastian. They will have the best luck in tracking down the number— Hello, little brother. I was wondering if you could come over and help me with a trace." Marc winked at her. "I'll make you waffles. They happen to be Jonny's specialty."

"I don't understand what's going on. Why are you calling your brothers here when I told you that I don't know where the house is? I got lost and turned around so much I don't know how to get back there." He nodded and handed her the bowl again.

"I have a tracer on the company phone as well as the phone from the service. When someone calls the office when we're closed, the service knows to let it ring three times before answering. And to always have to put them on hold, even if they know how to reach me. That makes it so the call doesn't have to be so long when I speak to the person and I can trace the call." She nodded as he handed her another bowl to mix. "Manning was on the phone long enough for me not just to be able to trace him, but to locate him too. And Sebastian is coming over to tell us just where Manning is."

"So you can find the house." He nodded. "You think he's not going to think of that?"

"Most men like Dawson never think that anyone is smarter than them. That's what makes catching them so much more fun. I love outthinking an asshole. Especially an asshole that hurt you."

They had waffles nearly done when Sebastian knocked on the door. He looked like a kid in a candy shop when Marc told him what he wanted. It was going to be a really long day, she thought.

CHAPTER 12

Sebastian watched Jonny. She was still really skittish around him, but he knew why now. She explained to him what his dad had said to her. And when she told him she was going to get him back and wanted to know if he wanted to help, it was all he could do not to pick her up and swing her around the room.

"It should be coming in soon." Marc nodded as he handed him another waffle. "I can't believe you had this thing all this time and didn't invite me over to check it out."

"It wasn't broken, and the point of having it was to keep it a secret. You would have told your nerdy friends and they'd be coming over too." Sebastian wasn't going to lie to him and tell him he wouldn't, but he didn't much care for the term "nerdy." Reed was the nerd, not him.

The signal bounced over the map. Then it began to slow and pinpoint where the call had come from. He looked up at Jonny when she sat down across from him. Marc had left the room to answer the phone in his office.

"You should know that I don't hate you." He nodded at her. "I don't know you, but I don't hate you. I'm…I never really had any family but my parents growing up, and I never dated. At all. I'm not very good around…I was going to say I'm not good around strangers, but I don't do well with people I know either."

"You'll be fine. We're not your usual family." When she snorted, he remembered what his dad had told him about her not knowing anything about her kind. "A family is also what a sort of pack of panthers is called. We just happen to be a family too. But ours is different. Most panthers want to live alone, especially males. We all live right here and have even built homes to be closer."

She nodded and stood. She was a pacer like Marc was. He wondered if they realized that yet. When the computer beeped that it was finished, she came around behind him and looked over his shoulder. But he noticed she was careful not to touch him. Standing quickly, he turned and pulled her into his arms. She didn't fight him, but was as stiff as a board.

"I won't hurt you." Marc came into the room just as he said that and leaned against the doorjamb. "See, he's not all foaming at the mouth. Relax. Hug me back. I promise you that I'm just a guy needing a hug from a beautiful sister-in-law."

"How did you know?" He lifted her hand with the large diamond on it. "Oh. We've not said anything yet. He asked me yesterday."

"And did you say yes?" Marc laughed at him. "What? She didn't fall down at your feet like Suzy Miller did?"

"Suzy Miller was seven, and I was all of nine. And no she didn't. I had to force her to sit still so that I could propose. And even that was a chore." Marc pulled her from him and hugged her. "Mine. Go find your own mate."

Sebastian sat down and looked at the address. "It's about fifty miles from here. Let me see if I can pull up any records on who owns it. And maybe a picture. Would you know if it was the same house if you saw it?"

"Maybe. When they brought me there, every time I was drugged. Then when I left, it wasn't usually by the front door. But it had a pool. I could smell the chlorine, so I always thought it was inside. And when I left, I could see that there were two other buildings behind the house. One of them looked like a barn, but I can't be sure. But it was large and maybe a couple of stories." She came around him when he asked her to look. "I don't…is there any way you can get to this part here? That's where I left from if this is the house."

Sebastian zoomed in on the left side of the house. He could make out a trellis as well as several small round little bushes under a large door. The decking that had come from the back extended just to the door.

"That's it. See this right here?" She pointed out the long white vine-covered trellis. "I used it to climb down. This room here is where he supposedly killed Anita. And those bushes are much larger."

Marc took the address and left to go to his computer. Jonny started clearing up the dishes. Sebastian watched her for several minutes before he spoke.

"You said every time. How many times did they take you?" She moved to the dishwasher with another load. "Jonny, please help me understand what we're going to be up against."

"Seven times. I got to be really good at getting away after the second time. It took me until then to realize they weren't very smart. I could stay on the property for hours at a time before I left. Usually they were all gone when I started off. But their way to keep me was getting to be much better, not the people holding me. The last time they captured me I was...." Marc sat down and told her to go on. "The last time they captured me I was leaving my job. Wasn't much of one, but it paid for my gas. Anyway, Roy walks up to me with Anita in his arms and a gun to her head. She was begging me not to let him kill her. As I tried to think what to do, I heard this other person—Henchman is what I'd begun to call Harris—he came around to my left with a gun. It wasn't until the first dart hit me that I realized it wasn't a regular gun. I didn't go down at first, but my cat sort of got pissed."

She stopped talking and looked out the window. He started to ask her what was wrong when Marc touched his arm. He put his finger to his lips and shook his head.

She seems to think things through better when she does that. It's kind of freaky, but it works for her. And what she said about being on the property for hours without them finding her is probably more than likely because she has a natural ability to stalk and hide. Last night and the night before, I couldn't find her in the woods no matter how much I tried. And let me tell you, I wanted to find her. She was like a fucking ghost. If she hadn't walked by me so that I could see her, I'd still be looking.

Sebastian looked at her with admiration. Marc was the best tracker of all of them, and if she outmaneuvered him then Sebastian was impressed. She turned to look at Marc, and Sebastian could see what Marc had meant. She got it. Whatever *it* had been, she got it.

"She said 'she'll pay now.' I just remembered that. 'She'll pay now,' then she said something about her brother was going to be avenged. I didn't know what that meant then or now, but she was in on it from the very beginning." Sebastian asked her who the woman was. "Anita Kidd. We met when I escaped a few years ago.

She'd moved into the building I was living in about a week later. She seemed so nice and friendly at first. Then as the weeks went by I realized she's nuts."

"Christ." Sebastian looked at them both. "She's none other than Anthony Kidd's daughter. You know who he is, the mob boss out of Jersey. She's reported to be worth millions and is…."

He read through the rest of the article, then stopped. This was not good. Not good at all. He clicked onto a few more pages before he spoke, no longer thinking about the couple in the room with him. When he was finished, he noticed first that he was in the kitchen alone and that it was nearly six hours later. He rubbed his hand over his face and went to find his brother and his mate. They were in the office going over something from Marc's investigative office.

"She really is nuts. According to some files I found, she's been in and out of asylums for years. Only until the past few years she hasn't. And it's more than likely because her father has stated that he's washed his hands of her. According to this report, she tried to kill him in a drunken rage and he was hospitalized for a month. She's not been able to see or be near him in almost four years. Her files say that she is bent on killing the one person who ruined her life."

"My mother, and since she can't find her, she's focused on me." Jonny started pacing again. "So Roy hooked up with her somehow, and now that they're partners, he and she both are trying to get me. I wonder if he knows what sort of person she is." Marc nodded. "She attacked him as well, right?"

"Not him but his office. He filed a claim that she'd went 'a little mad with grief' over something and had torn his office up. The insurance company didn't pay because it was dropped by Dawson a few days later. Probably because her dad found out and paid up." Sebastian pointed to the printer as he continued. "I sent some stuff to that one. If you had it on, you'd have been reading it by now."

"It turns off when I'm not using it. I asked you three times to fix that, and you kept telling me you'd get around to it." Marc turned on the printer and stood there as several sheets started spitting out. "Is this going to be more than five hundred sheets?"

"Close, but no." He laughed. "I wanted you to see some of the destruction she caused, as well as a few of her records I managed to get. Some places should have a better security system if they want to keep records off the grid."

They went over the papers as he watched them. Marc would read them, then hand them to Jonny. Sebastian was happy for them both, especially his brother. No one had ever dreamed that he'd find someone else. Sebastian was going to be the best mate he could be if he ever found his. He had been keeping mental notes on what he noticed his brothers did to both piss off their own mates as well as what made them smile. Jonny by far smiled the most.

"It says here that she's living in Jersey with her father. Do you have any idea where she really is?" Jonny asked. Sebastian nodded. "Let me guess, the house I was in."

"Yes. She's been there for nearly two years according to DMV records. Then last year she was supposed to get her licenses renewed but couldn't. It doesn't say why." He had an idea it had something to do with the hit and run she'd killed someone in and never spent any jail time over, but he would let them find that. "Jonny, I think you should learn to fire a gun. She's going to come for you, and the more prepared you are, the better chance you stand of living."

"No. If I take the bitch out, it's going to be by my own hands. She wanted my cat, so she's fucking going to get it." Sebastian looked at Marc. He looked as nervous as he felt. Jonny wasn't as timid as she first appeared.

~~~

Roy was ready to take what he had and leave the country. His latest dealings with Anita a week ago had ended with him being tied to his bed while she beat him with a whip and a bat. He shivered when he thought of what she'd done to him—all the things she'd done to him—and he shifted in his chair.

She'd walked into his office like she owned the place. He had been going over ideas on how to make it up to the people that were screaming at him and threatening him with a lawyer. His only solution was to simply disappear. He'd been about to tell her that when she came around behind him and wrapped her arms around his neck. Her affection soon turned violent and she slammed his head down on the desk twice before he lost consciousness. When he woke, he felt terror like he'd never felt in his life.

She'd gotten him to his bedroom. He had no idea how she'd done it, but there he had been. A gag ball had been strapped to his mouth, and he'd been naked and on his belly. He tried to jerk from the cuffs at his wrists and ankles, but all he managed to do was tear into his skin. He glanced down at the bandages there and knew that they covered nine stitches. It was nothing compared to his back and legs.

He had no idea how long he'd been in the room with her. He knew that there were times when he simply wanted her to kill him, begged her to hurt him. But she'd only hit
~~~

him more and harder, never once saying a single word to him the entire time. Every time he blacked out, he'd wake to find her lying next to him masturbating.

When he woke, as it turned out three days later, she was gone and he was loose. There was a note beside him, and he struggled to read it until finally things came into focus. His body was wracked with pain, and when he read her words, he knew that it was her or him. Reaching for the bedside phone, he'd called the only man he knew who could help him. An hour later, he was in a special hospital being treated. And Anthony Kidd was seated next to his bed the entire time.

"Can't do this again." Anthony nodded. "Have to leave before she kills me. If I don't, she'll kill me."

"I understand. And I'm sorry, Roy. But I'll take care of her. This is my mess and I'll take care of it. You simply wait for me."

Roy handed him the note he still had in his hand. He read it aloud.

"When I find my daddy dearest and get all his money, I'm coming back for you. Both of you will suffer much more than this little slapping around I've given you. Love you so much, A."

Anthony lowered his head and began to cry. Great sobbing came from him as he sat there with the note in his hand. The doctor at his back never said a word, but handed him a box of tissues and went back to work. Roy could only watch Anthony in stunned silence. When he lifted his head, Roy thought he looked like he'd aged ten years in just those few moments.

"I'll take care of this. You just let me know when you find her or she comes back to you. I'll have a team standing by. Also, you won't be able to live in this area for the rest of your life when I'm done. So you'd better have all your affairs in order before she gets to you. You're going to take the fall for killing her. It's the least you can do for me."

Roy nodded. And armed with a few hundred pain pills and a nurse to come by twice a day to change the dressing, he was sent home. The bedroom that he'd been held in was completely empty of everything, including his clothes. He found them in the room down the hall, dry cleaning bags still on them, and his other clothing in bundles on the bed. And something else he'd noticed; not one thing that belonged to Anita was anywhere in the house.

That had been two days ago and he'd not seen her since. There were others around the house now that hadn't been there before. The cook was new and wore a gun on her hip, and the men who worked in the yard seemed to trim the same bushes every day. He didn't care so long as they kept him from being killed.

Moving slowly, he went to the sofa in his office. He had to move like this every two hours or he got so stiff that he wouldn't be able to stand to piss. He was glad to see that his urine was a great deal less red now, and it didn't burn like he was on fire when he did. He sat on the sofa and took a pain pill. Christ, he was hurting.

The phone ringing startled him awake, and when he jerked, he cried out in pain. Sweat covered his body, and when he reached for the phone, pain tore into him. When he answered, he sat here for several seconds before what the woman on the other end was saying registered.

"Are you listening to me, Roy? I said do you want to make a deal? I want you out of my life and that of my parents, and if I do one job for you, will you leave me the fuck alone?" Jonny, Jonny had called.

"One job?" His voice cracked and he tried again. "You'll do one job and you'll do it the way I say?"

"Yes. But I want it in writing that if you come near me and my family again, I'll come for you." She sounded different, more confident. He wasn't sure he liked it, but he was desperate and could use the extra money she'd bring him.

"Yes, okay. You come here tomorrow and I'll have it all set up. Then when it's done I'll sign whatever it is you want." He tried to stand to go to his desk, but he had to hold on or fall. "Just let me get to a pen and some papers to get the number you're calling me from."

Something occurred to him, but he was in so much pain that it over-rode anything that might have filtered through his mind. As he shuffled to the desk, he heard her talking, but again couldn't concentrate.

"What the fuck is wrong with you? You sound like you're running a marathon or something. You were in better shape before you hooked up with Anita." He stopped moving. She knew. She knew was all he could think about.

"Anita? I don't know what you mean. She's just away on holiday, that's all. And when she gets back here, I'll have her call you."

"I saw you kill her." He started to deny it. Roy opened his mouth to tell her that he hadn't killed her, not yet at any rate. That her father had said he'd take care of it, when Roy remembered the day that Jonny had left.

"I didn't kill her. We were going to use that against you, try to get you to see reason, or I would scare you with it. But you'd left before I could. She's not dead." He laughed, then moaned in pain. "I wish to Christ she was, but she's very much alive."

"And you know why she came to you, don't you?" He told her he did. "Well, guess what, so do I. And I have enough on you right now to convict the both of you. You really should check your filing cabinet to see if it's locked before you let people run around your house without supervision."

The line went dead, and he ended the call. He looked at the filing cabinet where he kept everything. It was never locked, and as far as he knew never had been. She'd been through it, and even if she took simply one file, it would be enough to put him away for a very long time. Something his father had said to him many years ago came to mind.

"Son, the only advice I can give you if you want to earn money on the backs of other people is never keep a record. Because no matter who you think you can trust, no matter how safe you think you have it stored away, somebody sometime is going to get it, and when they do, you might as well put a bullet to your head, because you're going down."

Maybe he was, but he sure as hell wasn't going down alone. He turned on his computer and began compiling information. Not just on the scam he was running with the exotic pets, but everything and everyone he'd ever dealt with. And he ended it with the information on Anthony and Anita Kidd.

"Take that, you motherfuckers." He saved it to two discs, then put it on a thumb drive as well. The discs went into his safe, which he left unlocked, and the drive on his key ring. Someone somewhere would find it and they'd be hitting the jackpot. Roy Dawson was done making his peace.

CHAPTER 13

As soon as she hung up the phone she stepped out onto the deck. Marc started to follow her, but Jack stopped him. She nodded to Monica and Caitlynne as she went out to be with her. Jack was pretty sure she knew how Jonny was feeling.

"You did well. I'm thinking old Roy is pissing himself about now." Jonny didn't turn but kept looking out at the woods. "It'll be over soon and you'll look back on this as a bad dream."

"Is that what you do? Pretend that it was all a bad dream and it's not real?" Jack didn't answer because she liked Jonny and didn't want to lie to her. "I don't think you do that at all. I'm betting when I get up in the middle of the night and see you wandering around the house, you're thinking of every hurt that has been done to you and the people who did it."

"I do that, yes. But I'm not going to let it beat me. Every day that I can sleep a little better or a little longer without being woke from a dream, I feel like I'm winning." The door opened behind her, and she saw Caitlynne come out onto the deck as well. "You think any of us can live with every choice we've made?"

"I don't expect you do, but these people hurt what's mine." Jack was impressed with her answer. "And I'm going to make them pay."

"Will you be able to live with that choice, Jonny?" They both looked at Caitlynne. "Killing another being, panther or not, is a big decision. Even in the heat of the moment, a life or death thing, it's something you'll have to live with for the rest of your life. Do you think you can do that?"

"Hell yes." Caitlynne applauded her. "I don't want you to think this is going to be fun for me, but when I think of all those people he hurt and made suffer, I want to find him now and chew his arm off."

"This isn't the first scam that Roy Dawson has tried. It's had the least impact on the murder count, but not for lack of trying. We're pretty sure that once an animal has served his purpose, or sometimes when he wants out, Roy has them killed. I think that you were just lucky that you were just exotic enough that you brought him a great deal of money. Otherwise he would have killed you after the first time." Caitlynne handed her a file as she continued. "Ten years ago, Dawson was working for a smalltime dealer named Fletcher. He wasn't worth much in the large scheme of things, but he was getting there. Dawson decided he wanted it all instead of just a cut. What he didn't know was that the man was only a part of a huge picture, and he ended up working for a mobster for about two years. Just about the time the mob boy turned up dead, Roy was flush with a great deal of cash."

"What does this have to do with me?" Jonny handed her the file, and Jack opened it. "It's nothing to me who else he's killed. I just want him to stop what he's doing now, to me."

"Selfish but honest, I can live with that," Caitlynne said with a smile. "But what this has to do with you is this. Two days ago Dawson was treated by one of my informants. He nearly wet himself when Anthony Kidd picked him up at his home and took him to a warehouse. While he was there, he treated Dawson. Someone had beaten him really badly. A whip was used, as was a bat. He told Kidd that Anita had done it. And she'd not said a word why. Then Dawson hands Kidd this note, and after he reads it he starts to cry like a baby. My informant handed him a box of tissues, and he took it. Would you like to know what it said?"

Jack nodded, too, when Jonny did. This was huge, fucking huge. Anthony Kidd was the right-hand man to every dealer in the country. If he couldn't get you any drugs, then you fucking didn't need them. And when he said you were done, you were gone too.

"When I find my daddy dearest and get all his money, I'm coming back for you. Both of you will suffer much more than this little slapping around I've given you. Love you so much, A."

Jonny sat down and looked at both of them. Jack waited for Jonny to speak, and when she seemed to be in a trance, she looked over at Caitlynne, her new boss.

"Could have handled that a little better, I'm thinking." Caitlynne snorted. "You think, I don't know, maybe taking it down a notch or two might have been a little easier on her?"

"You think Roy will when he comes for her? And you and I both have been in this business long enough to know that he will. He'll have to. Or he'll send Anita after her. Either way, she's going to be in a shit-ton of trouble when it happens." She nodded, not agreeing with how she'd said it, but that she was right about Roy. "Besides, I think she'll come out on top. She's a kick-ass kid."

"And she's sitting right here." Jack grinned at Jonny. Yeah, she liked this girl. She was going to help her any way she could.

"So, you're going to marry Marc, right?" Jonny nodded. "Good, there are some things you should know about me."

The chair Jonny was sitting in began to rise. As it moved around the deck, Jonny didn't say a word but held on. When she sat her across from her, Jack reached into her mind and captured a small memory and smiled.

"You and Marc have been doing the nasty in the woods." The little push back didn't bother her so much, but when she felt her nose bleed, Jack stopped touching Jonny's mind. She looked at her and waited before she tried again. This time her head exploded in pain.

"Don't." Jack held up her hand to Caitlynne when she started toward her. "Can you do anything but that?"

"No. I can lift a few items but not very much, and sometimes when I'm PMSing, I can do a lot more, but not on the scale you can." Jack nodded at Jonny. "Oh, and I can hide really well."

"Hide?" Jack looked at Caitlynne when she asked. "What do you mean hide? My son can hide. Help me understand."

"I can tread really lightly on anything. Floors, ground, even leaves. I can move through anything like it's not there." Jack sat up and stared at her. "I didn't know I could do it until I had to escape the house and there were a couple dozen men around. They never saw me."

"Never saw you or never heard you because you didn't let them, or they just couldn't?" Jack went to the door and asked Dylan to come out. "Don't hurt him, but let him read your mind. He won't hurt you, but he can dig deeper than any of us can."

Marc came out with Dylan and she told them what she wanted. Marc went to Jonny and held her while Jack told him what she thought was happening. Marc started to nod.

"I've seen her do it. We were in the woods and I couldn't find her. I could smell her everywhere but not see her. She's really good. I've never seen a better tracker than her." Jack smiled. "I don't like that look. What are you up to?"

"Let Dylan see if what I'm thinking is going on." She nodded to Jonny. "You're not going to hurt him are you? Hurting me was okay, but this is—"

"You hurt her?" Jack stood in front of Dylan when he stood. He looked down at her, and she could see his cat. He was the sexiest thing she'd ever seen. Kissing her mate quickly on the mouth, she told him to behave.

Dylan sat down and glared at Jonny, but Jack knew he'd not hurt her. She wasn't so sure about Jonny, because, while she seemed to have some control over her power, it wasn't a great deal of it. Dylan closed his eyes and sat very still for several minutes. When his nose began to bleed, she started to tell him to stop. He held out his hand in much the same way as she'd done to Caitlynne. She knew she'd been right when he opened his eyes and looked at her.

"Incredible. She can manipulate your mind so that you can't see her even if you're standing right on top of her. She's able to make you think you can't hear or see her at all." He looked at her. "How do you do it?"

Jonny shrugged. "I just think that I'd be a lot safer if they didn't see me, and they can't. When Marc and I were playing in the woods, I could feel his frustration and…and I let him see me. I didn't want him to leave me again."

"I didn't leave you. I thought you'd gone back into the house." He kissed her. Jack felt her cat stir, and she turned to the woods. Someone was out there. Then she saw Dylan stand.

"Go in the house." Caitlynne had her gun out, as did Jack. Marc shoved Jonny behind him and shifted. She did as well, and Jack heard the door behind her open again and knew that the rest of the Bowens were also coming out. George and Corrine were standing in the doorway.

"What is it?" Jack said she didn't know, her voice as low as George's was. "I've sent the nannies to the basement near the door with the babies. Corrine and I are going to go in the front to see if there is anything coming from there."

She nodded and watched the tree line. A shadow of a person came into view, and Jonny growled low. Jack didn't move but reached out to the cat and spoke to her.

Go out there and think whatever fucking thought you have to so he can't see you. She leapt off the deck to do as she asked. Jack grabbed a handful of fur before Marc could follow her. *If she gets distracted because you're with her, you could get her killed. Stay right here.*

He growled, and she let him go. When he didn't move, she knew that he would heed her wishes. She'd pay later, especially if something happened to Jonny, but for now she could live with it.

The person kept coming toward them, and Jack could see that Jonny was standing right beside the person as he walked. When Jonny touched her mind, Jack nearly burst with happiness.

He's not armed that I can smell, and he does smell. Like a dog...no, a wolf and a... Is there such a thing as something that can be everything?" Jack told her it was a shifter. *Well, he stinks. And he...can you see him?*

Yes, and you as well. You're selective about who sees you apparently. Jack put her gun away when the man was within the light. "Everyone, I'd like you to meet Chris Reutter. He's a shifter I know from way back."

"Hey, kid. Wow, you sure hang with some impressive cats. I figured you'd be with a male, and here you are." He grinned when Dylan growled. "Your mate, I presume?"

"Yeah. What the hell do you want, and more importantly, how the hell did you get in here?" She watched as the others went into the house, no doubt to dress. Dylan didn't move from between her and Chris. Jack nodded her thanks to Jonny as she went by.

"I shifted to a hawk and flew over the fence. Nice system if you're only able to be two or four legged. But anyway, I'm here because there's this guy looking for you guys. A guy by the name of Kidd, know him?"

"Could. What's he looking for us for?" Chris walked up on the deck and bowed before Dylan. The two of them stared at one another for several minutes, and Jack was ready to hit them both. Males and their testosterone. Dylan nodded and went to the door and slipped inside the house.

"Nice guy. He's very much in love with you. He threatened me, did you know that?" She nodded. "Hum. He wants your family actually. He's got someone he wants dead, and he wants a few cats to do it."

"How did you find out?" Before he could answer, he was invited in the house by Corrine. Chris looked at her, then back at Jack. She nodded. She was too exposed out there, and turned to see Caitlynne still standing there.

"He's not nervous, nor does he seem to be lying, does he?" Jack shook her head at Caitlynne. "I'm pretty sure he's going to give us more than we have, and it's going to piss off Jonny more."

"Probably. But that's not necessarily a bad thing, is it?" Caitlynne shook her head. "I didn't think so either. Let's go see what he wants."

~~~

Walker and she were sitting at the table when Marc came in the room. She had been talking about his dad and how he'd tricked her. Walker was a good guy, and he never seemed to talk down to her. She liked this brother best of all. Walker smiled at Marc, and Jonny wondered what he was going to do.

"Jonny was laying out her plan to get back at Dad. I told her I'm all in. What do you think of it?" Marc looked at her, then Walker. "She didn't tell you, did she?"

"Not all of it, just the basic outline. Dad will have a shit when she does it to him. I can't wait." Walker nodded and left them alone. She looked up at him.

"You ready?" He nodded. "Good, because I'm not. Do you think that meeting him on his own turf is a good idea?"

"I don't just think so, but so do the experts. Caitlynne and Jack seem to think this is the best way to get him out of your life." He took her hand into his. "And I'm all for us getting on with our lives."

She nodded. She would be too. And to be able to live in one house would be nice instead of moving from one to the other all the time. They'd been bouncing between their house and Khan's for nearly the entire time she'd known him. Then there was Walker's house. They were going to go there for Memorial Day. She just wanted some quiet time.
~~~

"Where would you like to go?" His question startled her. "On our honeymoon. Where would you like to go? France, London, or we could take a long cruise."

"I don't know. I don't even have a passport or anything." She didn't have clothes nice enough to go to the picnic either, and when he lifted her chin up, she blurted that out to him.

When he stood up, he pulled her along with him. They were out the door and into his car before she could ask where they were going. When she asked him if maybe they ought to have said something to someone, he took out his cell and handed it to her.

"I don't know how to use this thing." She shoved it back at him, panicky, but he wouldn't take it. "I've had one before, but all it would do was ring and I answered. This one has more icons on it than I've ever seen."

"Just slide your finger across to the right. There at the bottom is a little thing that looks like a telephone. Press it." She glared at him, and he grinned. "I'm showing you how. Now slide you finger upward until you find Khan's picture. Once you do, press it and he'll hopefully answer."

"I really hate you right now." He laughed as the phone rang. Khan answered. "It's Jonny Thomas. I have your brother's phone and he's left your house. So have I, but we've left your…I'm so stupid."

Khan's laughter made her smile. "Take a deep breath and let's start again. I get that you're both not here. Should we hold dinner?"

She asked Marc. "He said no. I don't know where we're going. Perhaps you could have me ask him so he'll tell you and I'll know too."

"Yes, since I may have to go and bail you out of jail for murdering him—that might be helpful. Also, I can avoid that place if I decide to go out tonight. That way I can honestly say I wasn't there."

She turned to Marc. "Are all of you Bowens smart asses? Because I have to tell you, it grates on the nerves after a while."

Both men laughed, and Marc took the phone. "I'm taking her to Sables, then to dinner. You need me to get anything for you while I'm out?"

Apparently not. After the phone was handed back to her, she put it on the console and decided she wasn't going to ask who Sable was or where they were going for dinner. She was pissed. Again. She realized she spent a great deal of her time mad at him for one thing or another.

They pulled into the drive of a lovely looking home. It wasn't until they were nearly to the deck that wrapped all the way around it that she realized it was a shop. She turned to look at him when he turned off the car. He leaned against the door and watched her.

"I suppose you think that whatever is inside is going to make up for you dragging me away from helping with dinner and reading a bedtime story to little George." He nodded. "Fat chance. We were just getting to the part in the book where Wilber sees the web."

He got out and came to open her door for her. She got out and he pressed her against the car and nipped at her lobe. She got all melty inside and tried really hard not to let him see it.

"You be a good girl in here and let me do what I want. I'll make it worth your while." She looked at him suspiciously. "I swear to you nothing in here is going to hurt you."

"I've heard that from you before. You seem to think that anything you want me to do is not going to hurt me.

Maybe I liked being hurt." The words were out before she could censor them. "I didn't mean that the way it sounded, I swear."

Marc licked along her throat to her mark he'd put on her again that morning. She couldn't stop the moan any more than she could curl her hands into his hair. This man was lethal. And she was pretty sure he knew it.

"Are you sure? Because instead of taking you in here and buying you clothes, we could go back to our house and find out if you like to be hurt or not. We could even stop at a couple of much more fun shops to buy some toys if you'd like." She looked at the house and then back at him.

"I do need clothes really badly. You keep tearing them off me." He nodded. "But toys? What sort of toys were you thinking?"

He growled low and stepped back. "You are a very bad girl. And so you know, you're going to pay. Come on. If we don't go in now, we won't be."

She followed him in, stopped in the doorway, and simply fell in love. "Oh my. Oh my, oh my, this is beautiful."

CHAPTER 14

Roy was waiting for her. Jonny said she'd be at the restaurant at six and it was five minutes till. He knew she'd be right on time. She was for everything. "On the Dot Jon" was what some of the others had begun to call her. When he saw her coming toward him, he stood, and that's when he noticed the man with her.

He was extremely tall—but then standing next to him any man would be—and he looked good standing next to Jonny, like wedding cake toppers. His suit was expensive, probably worth more than Roy's entire closet, but it was the way Jonny looked that took his breath away.

She was wearing what he could only describe as amazing. A black dress that fit her trim body like it had been painted on her. Short, so that when she walked in those black high heels it looked like the length of her legs was twice that of her body. And damn what a body she had. He'd never noticed just how beautiful she really was. When the man pulled out the chair for her, Jonny sat down. Roy sat when the man did.

"I didn't know we were bringing company to this meeting, Jonny. I would have brought a date as well." She smiled at him, picked up her napkin, and put it across her lap without answering. The waiter came to take their drink order. She ordered a white wine, the man bourbon straight. Because of the pain pills that were running through his body, making this meeting possible, Roy declined and drank his water.

"I said I'd do this one gig and I'm done. You'll leave my family alone, and me as well. Are those the terms we agreed to?" He didn't like this Jonny. He wanted to bring her down a notch or two before she got out of hand.

"No, I said I would agree to this after you did the job. If the job doesn't net me what I wanted, why should I give you what you want?" The man stood and pulled out Jonny's chair. "Wait. What are you doing? I thought we would discuss this."

"A discussion, by the very definition of the word, means we talk about terms and we both come to some sort of agreement. You said you wouldn't give me anything until you got what you wanted. Not very fair if you ask me." She put her hand on the man's arm and started away, and Roy panicked.

"Come back here. I'll listen to what you want and be more opened-minded." She looked at the man and he nodded. "You know that it would be polite if you introduced me to your date. That would be a good beginning, don't you think?"

"Of course. Roy Dawson, this is my soon-to-be husband Marc Bowen. Marc, this is the man that I was telling you about. The thief." She picked up her glass, and he noticed the diamond.

"Christ, is that real?" Marc laughed and Roy felt himself flush. "I didn't mean to say that. I've been a little under the weather and I've been on pain pills for a while."

"Of course you have." Marc leaned back in his chair, and Roy felt sweat roll down his back. "You've been hurting my fiancée for a number of years now, and I'd like for it to stop. As of this moment, as a matter of fact."

Roy looked from her to him again. This wasn't going at all like he had planned. He started to say something else when another man sat down with them, bringing a chair from another table.

"Hello there. You're Roy Dawson, are you not?" Roy nodded. "Thought so. You're fucking up big time, buddy. There are rules you need to follow, and you've pissed in about a dozen leaders' shit and they are not happy."

Roy sat up straighter, even though it hurt like hell. "I'm sorry, but do I know you? We're trying to have a conversation here and you're being very rude."

"I'm Khan Bowen, the leader of the panthers in this area. When you asked a shifter to become one of us, you violated about ten laws. Then when you kidnapped my sister-in-law, you set my entire family on your ass. See?"

Roy looked around the restaurant and whimpered. They were cats. Every person in the room was a large cat. And not just panthers either. There were two Bengal tigers, one of them a snowy white. He looked back at Jonny and the two men.

"I…where did they come from? Where…are they all here with you?" Khan looked around the room, then back at him. Roy did the same. Everyone were people again, humans just like before.

"Are you all right?" Khan asked. Roy shook his head. "You look like you've seen a ghost. There are some people here that want to talk to you about this theft ring you got going on. None of them are very happy that you're making a profit off their subjects."

"No. No I don't want to meet anyone else." He stood up and then sat down when Khan barked for him to sit.

"Please, don't hurt me. I'll leave her alone. I swear this was going to be my last job anyway. I'll just leave as soon as I'm finished with Anita. I swear it."

"What thing with Anita?" He looked at Jonny. "I asked you what you are going to finish with Anita."

"Her daddy wants her killed. He wants me to let him know when she comes to the house again, and when she gets there, he is going to have his men come in. They're already at the house waiting. I can hardly take a shit without one of them coming to see if she's there yet."

Roy flushed when he realized what he'd just said. But she was looking at Marc again. He had a feeling they were talking about him but found he really didn't care. He just wanted out of there. He glanced around the room again, then back at the other man. When he winked, Roy thought for sure his eyes had changed, but didn't want to think about it. When Jonny looked at him again, he was relieved. Why on earth did he think this was a good idea? Jonny snapped her fingers in front of his face when she started talking.

"You're going to go home now and call me when Anita contacts you. I mean, the moment she contacts you. Then you can call whomever else you're supposed to." Marc stood up and pulled Jonny's chair out. "You contact me again other than for that and I'll...."

Her hand morphed into a paw, and claws dug deep into his flesh as blood pooled in the cloth beneath his hand where she held him down. She lifted her hand, and it was suddenly a human hand again. When he looked around the room, everyone was staring at him, but with eyes that seemed to glow in the restaurant lighting. He was done.

"I won't call you again. In fact, once I'm finished with Anthony, I'm fucking out of here. This place has gotten to be scary." Khan stood up, and right before his eyes, the man shifted.

Clothes tore from him and his skin furred. His mouth filled with an ungodly amount of sharp teeth. He realized at that moment he'd never had a cat this close to him. Not even Jonny had ever been this upfront in his face in all the time he'd made her work for him. Roy felt his bladder let go when the huge black panther licked his hand.

He sat there for a long time after they left, not moving to pick up his fork when his dinner arrived. He didn't remember ordering it, nor did he have a clue what it might have been. All he knew was that he'd wet himself, a panther had licked him, and he was seeing things. He tried to think, one thing at a time, about what had happened here.

As far as pissing his pants was concerned, and everything else for that matter, it was pretty fucking humiliating. Not the end of the world when he thought of what he could have done to himself…like crapping his pants for one, blowing his brains out for another. But he was still alive to fight…no, not fight. He was finished fighting.

The panther licking the wound that Jonny had given him was something else that freaked him out a little. He had watched as it healed in a matter of minutes instead of days. He had a hysterical thought that he should see how much he'd charge him to lick his back, but as soon as the thought entered his mind, he let it go. Having that many teeth where he couldn't see them might be bad. Another short burble of laughter escaped, and he put his hand over his mouth to stop it.

The people in the room being cats was next on his list. He couldn't quite put anything to that to make it right in his head no matter how hard he tried. Had he been drunk? Maybe. The pain pill, too, might have contributed to it, but he was pretty sure that hadn't been right either. They had made him see them as their natural state. That one had merit. He had a feeling that Jonny wasn't the only cat in the world, but having seen so many in one place was…it had been too much. Roy looked up as Harris came toward him and sat in the chair that Jonny had been in.

"Boss? I thought you'd have been out hours ago." Harris put his hand over his nose and looked around. "Someone wet their pants."

"That would be me." Harris looked at him oddly, then leaned in and sniffed. "Why would I lie about something like that? Bring the car around and see if there is anything to cover the seat with."

"You wet yourself?" Roy nodded. "What the fuck did you do that for? Did someone make you?"

"Yes. It's a new thing in terrorizing people in plush restaurants. They run in with a gun, hold it to your head, and order you to wet your pants or they'll blow your brains out. Sometimes they ask you to shit yourself, but I was lucky in that I only had to piss." Roy had a feeling that Harris was trying to figure out if he was kidding or not. "Go get the car."

"And Jonny? What we gonna do about her?" Roy shivered and thought about her claw cutting into him, the other panther licking it. He shook his head at Harris.

"Nothing. She's a dead end as far as anything goes. I'm out of the exotic animal business as of right now." He stood up with help and moved slowly to the front of the restaurant, leaving three hundred dollars on the table for the check and tip. "And Harris, I don't want you to ever mention her name to me again. Do you understand me? Not ever again."

Roy rode home on his suit jacket. It took him forty minutes to get from the front restaurant door to his bathroom, where he took off every bit of his clothes and put them into the trash can. By the time he was getting out of the shower, he was sobbing again. All this was Jonny's fault.

"But I'm not stupid," he told his reflection. "I'm not going after her, nor am I going to go after anyone in her family. I know for a fact that I'll live a great deal longer."

By the time he was getting into bed, Roy had a plan. Find Anita, help her get dead, and leave the country. He didn't even care if his house sat there for decades without anyone ever setting foot in it again. He was done. Closing his eyes, he let his mind drift on the double dose of pain medication he took. He saw cats big and small chasing him. But he smiled. Soon it would all be over.

~~~

Marc was carrying in the last of the bags when his phone rang. He put them down to answer. He leaned against the car to talk to his brother, knowing just what he wanted. He glanced up at the house and saw the bedroom light come on.

"How is she taking this? Any better than when we left Dawson?" Khan sounded as concerned as he was. "She took it pretty hard, didn't she?"

"Yeah, she did. I think thinking that your friend betrayed you and finding out for sure that she did would be a hard one for anyone to take. Christ, I wish I could make it all better for her."

"Monica said to give her a credit card and let her take her shopping. For a reason I can't think why, Jonny doesn't
~~~

strike me as a 'depressed clothes' shopper." They both laughed. "I would think that if you took her to a range to shoot something, she'd feel better."

He glanced up at the house again. "You know, I think you might be right. I still have that target thing set up in the back. I could take her out there and let her take her aggressions out on a few hundred bottles."

"Good. Now what are we going to do about Dawson and Kidd? There has to be something we can do to protect her. She's family." Khan laughed again. "That trick that Dylan did with the cats nearly made me laugh out loud when I saw the look on the fucker's face. Christ, he really thought the room was full of cats, didn't he?"

"I know. And he pissed himself when you shifted. What the hell, Khan, were you trying to cause a riot?" But it had been funny to know that his big brother could make a human do that.

"Dylan told me to. He said no one would notice. And they didn't. What did your mate do? She nearly took his hand off. How did you get her to stop?" He told him he pinched her tight. "Good job. I'm pretty sure she was going to take his wrist off if you hadn't. Poor girl."

Poor girl indeed. She was upset, and everyone in the limo had known it. Calling Dawson had been Caitlynne's idea. She said it would be something to make him remember she was a predator. The cats had been Dylan's. He'd wanted to scare the man who dared upset his newest sister-in-law. Khan wanted to show him the force of them all as a family, and Marc just wanted it over with.

"I should go get her. If you hear some gunfire, it'll be us. I need to get her mind off this, for a little while anyway." Khan agreed with him. "I have about a dozen leads on Anita. When I get them narrowed down to a few we'll see what we can do about finding her too. Kidd killing his daughter, does that sound right to you?"

"Yes and no. I think he probably wants her dead, but like Chris told us, he thinks he wants both of them dead, Dawson and his daughter. I'm thinking murder and suicide."

The conversation with Chris had been an eye-opener, and the reason for an impromptu meeting tonight. Caitlynne had wanted him off the grounds so she could see if what Chris had told them about the bodies was true. They hadn't heard from her yet, but Marc had no doubt that she was going to find a great many bodies on the man's property. He seemed to be just the type to kill when things weren't going his way.

"What about the rest? Have you been able to contact anyone else about some of their packs and such?" Khan, being leader, could contact other leaders, wolf, bear, and anyone else that might have had missing group members. "Someone, somewhere has to be looking for their child."

"I've gotten in touch with the local wolf pack. He said he has had some go missing, and he'll see if he can find out just how many. I'm still trying to find a local streak. According to Chris, there had been a great many tigers there before he found Jonny to replace them."

Chris had had files and files of records. He'd made copies of everything because the idiot that owned them had never locked it up. Chris was an informant for all sorts of government agencies, but also a really good friend of Jack's. That girl had a great many oddball friends.

They ended the conversation, and he picked up his bags. When he went into the house Jonny was sitting on their bed with all the clothes spread out around her. He sat the last two down and knelt in front of her, taking her hand.

"You okay, sweetheart?" She nodded and looked around the room. He did as well. There were bags and clothes on every surface.

"We might have gone a little overboard here." He laughed with her. "Where on earth am I supposed to wear all these to? I've never had so many clothes in all my life."

She picked up a blouse next to her and rubbed in over her cheek, then over his. It was silk and he loved it. He wanted to see it on her just for the purpose of him tearing it from her. He reached for the bright green little bra and panties that he'd picked out.

"If you go and put these on for me, I'll take you out back and let you shoot my gun." He wiggled his brows at her, and she laughed. "Then when we're all finished, I'll let you seduce me again. I sort of like that. Then there is the payback I owe you for getting me all worked up about toys."

She took the panties from him, wrapped them around his neck, and pulled them away slowly. She was doing it again. The woman had no experience with sex before he met her, and now he had a seductress. Christ, he was one lucky motherfucker.

"Get dressed in something comfy. We need to get you to the shooting range, and then I want to take you against the nearest tree." He stood and she ran her hand down his cock. "You keep that up and there will be no way we'll leave this bedroom."

"Is that supposed to be a threat?" She leaned her cheek into him and moaned. "You're very hard, aren't you? It's a small wonder that you can walk around and not be dizzy. Is all your blood always pooled right here?"

"Only when you're around." When she reached for his belt, he knew that he should stop her, but he couldn't. "Jonny, we really should be going outside and—"

She tore his jeans from him. Then his boxers. When she fisted his cock and took him to her mouth, he lost all train of thought but what she was doing to him. His last thought was that he'd take her tomorrow after work. Then she touched his balls and he was gone.

CHAPTER 15

Anita looked out the hotel window. She'd been there for nearly a week now, and she was bored. She glanced over at the man on her bed, trying to remember where he'd come from, but drew a blank. He'd been a great way to end her shitty night last night, but now she just wanted him gone. Going to the bed, she slapped him in the face.

"Get out." He looked at her like he wasn't sure what she'd said. "I said to get the fuck out. I'm finished with you, and unless you want rolled into a sheet and tossed into the dumpster out back, I would suggest you get out now."

She found his pants and tossed them at him as he sat up. Then she picked up his shirt and underwear. Anita held them up. Tighty-whities? What grown man wore those anymore? She threw them at him as well. Finding and throwing his shoes at him made her laugh. He wasn't very fast on his feet, it seemed. When he was pulling on his pants, holding onto all his stuff, she went to the door and held it open for him.

"You really are a fucking cunt, aren't you?" She smiled at his question. "Your loss, bitch. I'm better in the morning."

"I should hope so. You weren't any good last night, that's for sure." Before he could say anything, she slammed the door in his face. She walked back to the bedroom to get a shower when her phone rang. She looked at the caller ID and ignored it. Daddy was on her shit list too.

To think he wouldn't let her come home when she'd left Roy's house. She was remembering bits and pieces of what she'd done to poor Roy, but not all. She still had no idea what had set her off. She'd been violent like that before, more than that really, but didn't have any idea what he'd done to her to make her so pissed. And then when she'd ended up at some bus stop with blood on her hands, she had called her daddy. He hadn't answered her the first day, and when he had on the second, she'd asked him for help.

"Do you know what it cost me to have him taken care of?" She'd asked him if he'd killed him. "No, I did not. I helped the poor bastard. Good God Anita, you nearly killed the man. He had nine broken ribs, more cuts on his back than the doctor could count, and you damaged his kidneys. If he doesn't need a transplant after this, it will be a miracle. The man is going to be sick for a very long while."

"So? It's not my fault. He must have done something to make me so mad." She hadn't known then and still didn't as yet. "I don't know why you didn't just let him die. It would have been a lot better for him in the long run. Especially for me. You want to make me happy, don't you, Daddy?"

He didn't say anything. The smile she'd had had faded. This wasn't what she had expected from the man who had given her everything. That was until that whore had killed her brother. Jonny was going to pay for the sins of her mother, she'd thought then, and had thought since she'd figured out that Jonny was Deb's daughter.

He asked her what she wanted. "I want to come home. I want to be with you for the rest of our lives together. You have said a great many times that we need to be there for each other, that we're all we have. Well, I think you're right. I want you to let me come there and stay."

She'd began throwing her things back in the suitcase she'd brought with her as she waited for him to tell her that he'd let her and was sending the car for her. She had just been ready to drag it out the door when he finally spoke.

"I don't think that's a good idea. I have a great many people coming in and out of here all the time, and I don't think having you here in the state you've been in lately will be conducive to business. You stay wherever you are and I'll…I'll send you some money. But coming here is out of the question."

She waited for him to tell her he was joking. Not that he'd been much of a kidder, but she waited all the same. She sat down on the edge of the couch, terrified for the first time in her life of her daddy.

"But, Daddy, I'm your little girl. You have to let me come home. I'm all the family you have left." He told her no again, and anger surged though her. "You'll regret this. Mark my words, Daddy dear, you will regret this."

"There are a great many things in my life I regret, Anita. More than a normal man should have, but this will never be one of them. You are not to step foot on any property that I own, or so help me I will have them shoot you on sight. You need help. A great deal of it, but I'm not going to help you anymore. You're on your own."

The call ended, and she sat there for nearly an hour before she realized she had nowhere to go and no one to help her. Going to the bedroom again, she put her clothes away carefully and crawled into the bed. She had been there until yesterday.

Getting out the shower, she dressed with care. She noticed that she was shaky and went to the mini-bar. There was always something there to give her a pick-up. She pulled the bottle of vodka out and began drinking straight from the bottle. This was what she needed.

By the time she remembered that her daddy had called, she was starting on the bottle of something brown. She couldn't read it and swore that someone had messed up the label so that she would think she was drinking top shelf when it was only watered down cheap shit. She staggered to her phone and tried to see the numbers and pressed one, hoping it was her daddy. It wasn't, it was Roy.

"What do you want, Anita? I really don't want to talk to you. So whatever you feel you have to say, say it. I'm finished with you." She tried to remember why he was so mad and gave up. It didn't matter to her anyway.

"Where she at? I want you to tell me." It didn't come out right, so she tried again. "That whore's daughter? What did you do with her?"

"What are you talking about? Jonny? How the hell should I know where she's at? You're supposed to be such great friends with her, you tell me." She tumbled off the bed and onto the floor. "Are you drunk already? Christ, Anita it's only ten in the morning. Do you have no respect for yourself at all?"

She wanted to tell him it was none of his business but thought she'd just mess it up. Instead, she tried to think why he'd called her. She could only think of one reason why he would and smiled.

"You want me to come back to you, don't you? You sly devlin…dental…. You're too sly. I'll come back on one…." The word escaped her. "You send me a car and I'll let you take me back."

"Take you back," he shouted in the phone. The man was happy, she could tell. Nodding, she made herself dizzy and held her head.

"Yes. But you have to be nice to me from now on. I don't want to have to…what happened to us? We were so happy." She laid her head on the floor to steady it. Man, she was really feeling great. "Did you make me mad at you, Roy Boy?"

"I most certainly did not." He was quiet for so long she nearly fell asleep. "You can come here and we'll talk. Just talk. I'm not saying I'll let you stay afterwards, but we can talk. Can you be here at around six tonight?"

"I can be there with big old bells on." She started humming a bell tune she'd heard somewhere. "Bells on my toes and ears. I'll even put them on my nipples if you want. Will that make you happy, Roy Boy?"

"Just be here to talk at six and forget the bells. I don't want to ever have sex with you again. You're a danger even to yourself, and I don't want anything to do with you like that again."

She stayed on the floor with her eyes closed. He said that now, but when she got there, she'd show him. He loved her, and as soon as he figured it out, things would go so much better for him. Smiling, she felt herself drift off and thought about what she'd wear tonight. She'd get up early and go find something sexy and tight. That would change his mind soon enough.

~~~

Jonny stretched over Marc. He held her, but she could tell that he was wasted. So was she. The man was absolutely wonderful in bed. For that matter, anywhere he
~~~

took her. She looked up at him and marveled that he was all hers.

"You do know that we're never going to get anything accomplished if you don't keep your hands off me?" She laughed at his statement. He didn't sound the least bit upset over it.

"Yes, well I needed to relieve your tension so mine could go away too." She laid her head on his chest. "She was never my friend, was she?"

He pulled her up even with his face and rolled her to her side and him with her. "No, baby, she wasn't, and I'm sorry for that. She is really sick in the mind. You heard what Dylan said she'd done to Roy. She beat him nearly to death."

Dylan had wanted her to understand that Anita was nuts. She had kinda figured that out on her own, but he had been right to tell her. But it still hurt to know that she'd been so sucked in by her.

"I think we scared Roy too." She laughed. "I've heard of people being scared enough to wet themselves, but I've never known anyone to actually do it."

"Yeah, me either. And you were amazing. I've never known anyone with such control over their cat before. How did you do that with just your paw?"

She held her hand up and morphed it again. Just to the wrist like she'd done in the restaurant. She made it human again and looked at him.

"When I was trapped and there were people around, I had to sometimes resort to other means of getting away. This worked for me." She snuggled back into chest. "Do you suppose he'll call us if she shows up?"

"He'll call. And when he does, we'll go and find out what the fuck it will take to make her back off." He held her tightly. "And if that doesn't work, we'll resort to other means."

She reached for her new phone when it rang. She looked at the caller ID and looked at Marc. He grabbed his phone and called Sebastian. It took her a few seconds to remember how to open it and answered a little too sharply.

"She call you too?" Jonny frowned at the question. "Anita. Did she call you too? She just called me wanting to move back in. I told her to be here at six so we could talk. Is that what you wanted?"

"Yes." She looked at Marc when he nodded. "She thinks you're going to let her move back in with you? You think that's such a good idea? I mean, she already beat you to shit, what's to say she won't kill you next time?"

Jonny didn't really care, but they wanted her to keep him on the phone to make sure he was still at his house when the troops arrived. Caitlynne had men on standby to go in and take care of all the men on the property that Kidd had placed. That's who Marc had called.

"I didn't say she was moving in, I said she wanted to talk about it. She won't get within ten feet of me again. Not so long as I can be armed. She's only going to be alive so her daddy can take care of her, and then I'm fucking out of here."

Good luck with that, she wanted to tell him. "We'll be there around five so we can arrive before she does. All we want to do is get her to back off like we asked you to do."

His laughter sounded strained, and she smiled. "You're fucking right I'm backing off. I would like to keep all my parts just where they are. Who the fuck knew there were more panthers in the area than you? I thought for sure you were a freak of nature. Turns out there are a shit-ton of you fuckers."

"Who knew you fuckers were so easy to scare piss-assed stupid." She looked over at Marc when he laughed. She felt a smile creep across her mouth, too, but she needed to stay hard-assed.

"I'm on medications, and some of the side effects are bladder control. I'm in a great deal pain all the time. You should see what she did to me."

There was desperation there, and she wanted to tell him she was sorry, but she wasn't going to lie to him no matter how badly she felt for that one second. Snorting, she decided to go for the throat, so to speak.

"I wonder how long it will take them to get that smell out of those leather seats. Or do you suppose they just tossed them out like you probably did your suit. I, of course, would be wearing adult diapers if I knew the meds I was taking made me piss myself when I was a scared little boy."

"You fucking cunt." She laughed at him. "I wish to Christ I would have let Anita kill you when she wanted to. Then you'd be dead and I'd be a happier man."

"No, you wouldn't, Roy. Men like you are never happy. There is always something there that you have to have, no matter who owns it or how much it costs. Mark my words, in a few weeks after this is over, you'll be into another scam, thinking it's going to make you a millionaire."

He hung up on her, and she looked at Marc. "Damn," Marc said, "remind me to never piss you off. You're good."

He pulled her into his arms and told her that he was at the house and that Caitlynne's men were on their way. And the trace on the phone would let them know what he said when he called Kidd.

"We'll leave here around three. That way we can be there by four. Caitlynne says that if this goes down like she hopes it does, there's a fat reward for you. She said you'll be known as the woman who brought down Anthony Kidd."

"I don't want a reward for that scum bag." She then thought of something. "How much?"

He laughed. "I don't know. Greedy are you? All my money isn't good enough, now you have to have more?"

"No. I was thinking of my mom and dad. They could get it. I mean that would be a good way for them to retire if it's enough maybe. They don't have to know it's from me. Caitlynne can swing that, can't she?" He nodded. "If nothing else, it will be enough that he could find a job later."

"It'll be enough. We'll make sure of it." He kissed her. "I love you. Very much. But I have to get to the office. I've been putting it off long enough. Want to come with me?"

She wanted to, but his mom had made arrangements for her to help her interview a cook and housekeeper. She told him that, and he smiled. She looked around the room and noticed that it was as messy as the kitchen.

"I'll work on this room before they get here. I'm sorry I'm such a slob. I told you that I—" He put his hand over her mouth.

"I'm just as sloppy as you. And most of this mess is the stuff we bought yesterday. You pick it up and we'll get it all washed tomorrow." He got out of the bed. "Also, I forgot to tell you, I bought you a car. It's in the garage with mine."

She sat there for several seconds before she got up to run and see what he'd gotten her. She had to come back twice. Once because she was naked, and the second time to find her shoes. It was pouring rain.

The car was a bright cherry red. And it was beautiful. She couldn't believe he'd gotten her one, and when she ran her fingers along the hood, she fell in love with it. She knew less about cars than she did about cooking, but had a feeling she would have to learn to curb the immediate desire to drive it really fast all the time. She was still looking at it when he came out with his briefcase and coat.

"I thought you'd be long gone out, trying to race unsuspecting cops on the road." She giggled at him. "You like it?"

"I love it. Oh my, it's so pretty, isn't it?" He nodded and rolled his eyes. "I know you think I should be impressed with the horse power or some such nonsense, but it's so red."

"Red. You like it because it's red? Okay then, you enjoy your red car. I'm going to work. What time is Mom supposed to be here?" She told him ten. "Well, you'd better get to work then or you'll never be dressed in time."

She looked at her watch and ran to the house. She came back and threw her wet body against his. He was laughing when she went to the house. She decided to tackle the kitchen first, then the bedroom. It was nearly two hours later when she had the last dish put away. Jonny decided that having someone do this for them would be better. She looked at the mess she'd made when she'd dropped two of the plates. Yes, much better.

The living room looked better but not great. Picking up his files, she took them to his office and laid them on the chair so they couldn't be seen from the doorway. Then she hit the bathroom down there and made her way up the stairs. Sheesh, she was exhausted, and all she'd done was spot clean. Moving to the bedroom, she stopped in the doorway.

He'd cleaned it up and made the bed. She found a note on the counter in the bathroom. She kissed it and put it into her pocket after reading it twice. "I made the bed and put your things in with mine in the drawers. I will think of them having mad sex all day, then come back there and jump your bones. I should be home around noon. Have fun with Mom, and don't growl at our new cook if you hire one. I love you, Marc."

The man was simply romantic.

CHAPTER 16

The stage was set, so to speak. Marc looked at his brother again and wished it would simply be over and done with. There were so many things that could go wrong, and having his brothers there in harm's way was making him twice as nervous. Then there was his Jonny.

"She's going to be fine, you know." Marc nodded at Khan. "She's a lot stronger than any of us give her credit for. Christ, she was in there talking to Caitlynne like she was in charge."

Marc laughed. "She said if her ass was on the line, she wanted details. I'm surprised that Caitlynne let her talk to her that way. She was a little snippy even with Mom."

"Yeah, but Mom gave as good as she got. And you saw the way she looked at her. Mom loves her very much." Marc nodded. "You guys are great together."

"I know." He looked at Khan. "Can I tell you something I'd never say to anyone else?"

"Of course. But I think I know what it is. Reed and I were talking with Walker about you guys. You love her more than you ever did Sonya, don't you?"

"Yes. And I don't think I would have…I would have loved her, but I doubt that we would be having this much fun. Sonya was…I feel really horrible saying this, but she was perfect for me at that time. But now I need more, want more, and Jonny gives it to me. She's amazing."

A car pulled up the drive, and they watched as a large man got out of the back of the limo. A voice cracked in his ear, and Marc watched the man as Caitlynne told them who he was from her point on the roof.

"That, my dear brothers, is the man himself. Anthony Kidd. I had hoped he'd show and we were right. This is going to be much better than just arresting a woman, we got the big guy."

Marc thought of the reward for Jonny's parents and knew that it was going to be big enough for them to live very well for the rest of their lives. He had told Caitlynne what Jonny wanted and she said she'd help as well. This was going to make Jonny very happy, if everything went as planned. Looking at his watch, he saw that Anita should arrive in about forty minutes.

The crew that Kidd had placed on the property was being taken out now. Her men, Caitlynne's, had moved into position yesterday, and they were to wait until Kidd came on site before they made their move. There were eighteen men now on their side, and six others sitting in the backs of cruisers.

He looked in the window where Jonny and Roy were sitting. The little camera that had been installed while Roy had been with them two days ago was working well. And the little laptop was something he'd brought so he and Khan could keep an eye on things. Marc was leaving nothing to chance.

"Hello. What are you doing here?" Anthony stood in the doorway and glared at Roy. "You said nothing about others being here. How did she come to be here before me?"

"Smarter?" Marc sighed and wondered if she'd ever curb her tongue. Then realized that he was glad she didn't. He loved her mouth and what it did to him. Shifting on his feet, he tried to concentrate on what was going on.

"You'll not use that tone with me, young lady. Do you have any idea who I am? I could have you killed in an instant." She nodded at him and patted the chair next to her.

"Before we get all shitty with each other, perhaps we can have a little talk about your involvement with your daughter's murders." Kidd had started forward, then stopped to look at Roy. "Oh, he didn't know about all of them. He does know about her attempt on my life. He was there, you know."

"I have no idea what you're talking about. If this is your idea of a joke, I'll have you know that having one more on my supposed list of crimes won't bother me the least bit. And no one would miss some little nobody like you anyway." She tisked at him. "You think that I came here unprepared? Think again. I never go anywhere that I don't know the ins and outs of everything going on."

"Good for you. But you've changed the subject. I was speaking about Clarence Shane and William Holbrook. The two men that you had buried in the garage of your new building? Sloppy work, that. They were both dug up this morning." She looked down at the empty file in her hand. "Will they find more, you think?"

The man who had shown Kidd into the office was Dylan. He'd taken the man's coat and had brushed against him. He was feeding the information to Jonny and she pretending to know. This was the part that scared Marc the most…a known killer in the same room with his smart-mouthed mate. This could go very badly.

"You think you have something on me, little girl? You have nothing. If you did, the police would be here and not just you. What are you doing here anyway? I don't believe you have any input in this."

"Oh, but there's were you're wrong. I have plenty to say. Like the money you stole from the National Bank on Tenth a week ago, and the five men you had killed when they failed to get out without getting the safety deposit boxes open. Or the two men you have rotting in your pool house." She shook her head. "I have plenty more if you want to hear it, but if you're willing to shut up and sit down, I'll tell you what I want in exchange for the information your daughter gave to me."

"Exchange? My daughter wouldn't have given you a damned thing." Kidd looked over at Dawson and grinned. "Is this your idea of a joke? It's not terribly funny if it is. You should have told me that you were going to waste my time like this."

"I had no idea what she was…. You have to know that I didn't do this. She's here because your daughter threatened her too. She just wants to talk to Anita. This is the daughter of the woman who killed your son."

Crunching gravel had him turning. Marc looked as a cab pulled up in front of the house and a woman got out. He almost didn't recognize her from her pictures they'd found on the Internet. Christ, she looked like she was in her late fifties instead of her mid-twenties. Caitlynne spoke in his ear.

"Is that Anita?" Her shock was evident. "Well, she should be the poster child for doing alcohol and drugs and why not to do them. She looks like she's been rode hard and put away wet to rot. Good Christ, she's nasty looking."

Khan laughed. Marc watched the woman stagger to the front door, where Dylan was again. They watched from where they were as he took her purse and laid it on a table and then walked away. Both he and Khan moved toward the door to get into position on the inside. Caitlynne said that she was moving as well.

The door to the office had been left open just enough for them to go in when needed. Marc moved to just on the other side so he could see in and watch for Khan. He was making his way to the other entrance on the other side of the room. That door had been left open earlier by Dylan. When he saw his brother, they both shifted and waited. They were as ready as they could be. Christ, he hoped this went as planned, but had been on enough of these to know they never did.

As soon as Anita walked in the room, he knew for a fact this was going to end badly and tensed himself for whatever happened. Dylan walked up behind him and touched his shoulder. He turned to look.

He had her purse. Anita's purse was in one hand and a Glock in the other. Marc felt as if ten years had been taken off him. Christ, he'd disarmed the mad woman. He nodded at his brother and watched as he shifted too. He knew that Reed, Dylan, and Sebastian were just outside the large window, and that Walker was in the room next door in the event that they needed his medical help. His family was there for him.

He listened to the happenings in the next room, feeling just a little better about how it might end.

~~~

Jonny watched the woman she'd considered her friend walk in the room. She looked stoned. Not only that, but she also reeked of liquor. A quick glance at the other two men
~~~

in the room confirmed that they were just as shocked as she was about Anita's appearance.

Her clothes didn't seem to fit her, and her blouse was on inside out. The skirt she had on was a deep coral color, and her blouse was a bright green. Jonny had no idea what she had done to her hair, but it looked as if she was trying for something along the lines of a rats' nest and had succeeded at it. Her shoes probably explained some of the reason she was staggering; one was a nice-heeled pump, the other a tennis shoe.

"Daddy, I didn't know you were going to be here. I'm so glad to see you." When she stepped forward to more than likely give him a hug, he stepped back. "You're not happy to see me? I can't believe you're still mad at me for that little tiff, are you?"

"What the hell have you done to yourself? You look…Christ, Anita, you look cheap. And drunk. Have you no shame to go out looking like this?" She looked down at her clothes, then up at her father. She didn't seem to have a clue what he was talking about.

"I dressed up to impress Roy here into taking me back. I think I look very nice." She looked at her shoes when she stumbled again. "Oops. I forget to change them both."

Her laugh was maniacal and manic. She looked over at Jonny, just noticing her, and glared. She reached for something on her arm and turned in a full circle, nearly tumbling over in the process.

"Where is my gun?" She looked around and mumbled something about her purse before her father spoke again.

"You brought a gun here? You can barely walk. What the fuck were you planning to do with a gun in your possession? Shoot yourself?" Anthony sat back down and looked at Roy. "I've changed my mind. You can deal with her."

Before Roy could say anything Jonny stood up. "Hello, Anita. You're supposed to be dead. But I guess that was a lie as well."

"I think you should remember your place, little bitch." Anita slipped to the couch and nearly fell over onto it. "I am twice the woman you'll ever be. And when I take care of business here, I'm going to be rich too. Daddy will make sure of that for me."

Jonny glanced in Anthony's direction and then back at Anita. "I don't think your daddy is going to help you with anything. But I did tell him what you told me about the bodies in the parking garage."

Anthony glared at her, then looked at his daughter. She watched as Roy made his way to the side door. He wasn't going anywhere and she knew it. As soon as she heard the low growl, she watched him stagger back into the room. When he looked at her, she winked.

"You told this woman about our business? Personal business that you caused to happen?" He stood up and began walking toward her. "I should have known better than to say a fucking word to you, Anita. You've been nothing but a problem since your brother died."

"She caused all this." Anita pointed at her. "This is all her fault because her mother was a whore and a slut."

"You have no idea what you're talking about. Your brother was a stupid fool who thought robbing a bank would be a blast. I paid those witnesses to say that he had helped them out. When he was killed, he was raping a woman in the back room with a gun to her head. He wasn't the saint that you've made him out to be."

"No. No, that's not right. He saved those people and she shot him." Anthony was shaking his head. "You lie. You'll say whatever you need to say to get what you want. Stop this now."

The gun was out and in Anthony's hand before Jonny could say anything. The first shot went off, then two more before she realized that she was being taken to the floor by a large cat. Khan commanded her to lay still.

He weighed her down, and she saw Marc flash by her. More shots were fired, and she closed her eyes when she heard a cat scream. Trying to get out from under Khan, he snarled. She shifted under him and tossed him off her.

Marc was hurt, but she couldn't tell how badly. Reed was standing over him, and Roy was pointing a gun at both of them. She moved up in front of Roy and reached for Khan.

Get them out of here, please. I can't let anyone get hurt because of me. Another shot was fired, but she didn't look to see who had been shot. She watched Roy. When he raised his weapon to fire at one of the men behind her, she leapt at his throat.

The world seemed to fade and come back to her. She saw Marc standing over her, cussing the air blue around him, and then Walker. Walker was smiling, and she wasn't sure why that made her feel better, but it did. He said something low, and she nodded, not sure why.

Opening her eyes, she saw Marc again, and he was holding her hand. She tried to talk to him, but her mouth refused to work. He told her he loved her and that if she died he was going to kick her ass, but she faded again. Things were fuzzing all the way around her.

She looked up the next time to see that she was in a bed. Marc was sitting next to her in a big chair and he was asleep. She turned her head when she heard someone clear their throat and saw her mom sitting on the bed.

"He's been there for two hours. Won't leave you because he said he's going to beat your ass when you wake. He said that if you shift you'll heal faster. Is that true?" She nodded at her mom. "You scared us all."

"Is he hurt?" Her mom shook her head. "I thought he was bleeding. I was so terrified when I saw that blood on his chest."

"It was on my shoulder, and I shifted." She looked at Marc. "What the hell were you thinking? You could have been killed. I thought Khan told you to stay still."

"Don't you dare take that tone with me. I was trying to save your sorry ass. What were you doing getting shot in the first place?" She sat up in the bed when her mom stood. "You think I couldn't handle myself? I had it under control, you pompous ass. Do you think that you're the only panther in the world that can be brave? I will let you know when I need—"

He tossed her back on the bed and kissed her. His hands seemed to be everywhere at the same time, and she moaned when he cupped her breast. The door clicking closed had her reach up, wrap her arms around him, and pull him closer. When he lifted his head, she looked up at him.

"You scared me." She nodded, knowing how he felt. "When that idiot shot you, I lost it. Will you never do anything like that again?"

"I'll try." He pinched her nipple. "Ouch. That wasn't necessary, was it? I'll promise you if you do the same for me. Seeing you there was the scariest thing I've ever seen."

She winced when he ran his other hand up her ribs. He rolled to his back and she could see that he was aroused.

His cock was filling out his jeans very nicely, and she wanted him. She reached for him only to have him grab her wrist to stop her.

"Don't. There are a number of people down in our living room wanting to talk to us. They want to know how you came to be in the house where three people were killed."

That had her sit up quickly. She wanted to ask him how, but he shook his head again. "It's best if you don't know anything until we get downstairs. We told them you were there to get your belongings from Roy and that the other two showed up after. Caitlynne is telling them that when she rolled in with her men that you were bleeding in a corner and that the other three were dead."

"So they're dead." He nodded and helped her up. "And you guys weren't there? I was there alone when it went down."

"Yes. No one is alive to dispute your word. Caitlynne is telling them that your parents told her about Roy and his meeting with Kidd. The daughter showing up had been a surprise. Jack took care of the rest. Did you know she has no fingerprints?"

Nodding, she went down the stairs with him holding her. She felt stupid and told him so, but he said that she was shot and that they needed to believe that. She sat on the couch and looked at the men in the room. Caitlynne and another man she didn't know were sitting with her.

And so the questions began. Five hours later, she was hurting and wanted to just take a nap. When the man with Caitlynne stood up, so did all the other men. He looked down at her and smiled before turning to the men.

"I think Mrs. Bowen has had enough, gentlemen. She's told you all several times why she was there and what she remembered. If anything, we should be thanking her for what her family did for us, not bombarding her with endless questions." He turned to her again. "On behalf of the President of the United States and me, we want to thank you for what you did for the country. Having a man like Anthony Kidd off the streets is one step closer to having safe towns again." Each man shook her hand as they left. She turned to Caitlynne when the room was empty of everyone but her, Marc, and herself.

"Who the hell was that?" Caitlynne started laughing, and Marc joined her. She sat back down, feeling very murderous toward them both.

"That was Marshall David, personal assistant of the president." Caitlynne sat down and stretched out. "You're all right there, Miss Thomas, so when is the wedding?"

CHAPTER 17

"I need for you to tell me what happened." Marc looked at her over their dinner table. "I keep having these odd moments when I think I remember something, but I'm not sure."

"What do you remember?" She shook her head at him. "Okay. How do you want this? Me pissed when I get to the part where you stepped in front of a bullet aimed for me, or the version where I try to think about how you saved mine and my other brother's ass?"

"The second one, please. And I remember the part up until I was standing in front of Roy, but I sort of…." She played with her pork chop. "I killed him, didn't I?"

He'd been waiting for her to ask. Walker and Khan had both told him not to tell her unless she asked him. He'd wanted to tell her how he'd been impressed with her and how much he loved her for saving him, but he'd waited. And now that she was asking, he wasn't sure he wanted to tell her.

"Yes. You killed him and Anita." She looked up once, then back down. "If you want this, I need for you to look at me. I'll feel better about telling you if I can see your face."

She looked up at him and then down. He waited, knowing that her need to know was going to override her fear of knowing. When she looked back at him, she looked like she was ready, but he could still feel her terror.

"You were standing in front of Roy, facing him. I don't think he could see you, because he kept telling Reed to get the fuck out of his way, that you were going to pay. He never really said for what, just that he was going to make you pay by taking away the one thing you loved." She nodded as if she remembered that. "But then he lifted his gun and you leapt at him. I don't think he ever saw you. But he knew that you were there. You knocked him back on his backside, and he screamed. He'd landed on a broken chair, and it had come up through his arm."

"I remember the smell of his blood. It was…it was as if it was tainted with something. Like…it was his drugs he had in his system. When I bit him, I could taste them too. I knew that if he got back up, we were all going to be dead. I had his throat in my mouth when there was…. I don't remember the next part."

He picked up his dish and hers, taking them to the dishwasher. Their cook and his wife, their new housekeeper, were starting tomorrow morning, and they'd been talking about them until she'd brought up the house and Roy. He loaded the dishes in the washer after scraping them off. He took a deep breath.

"Anita struggled with her dad when he pulled out his gun. Dylan and I had come into the room about then, and he'd been knocked on his ass by the couch coming back at him when Anita stood up and tumbled back. Her dad had fallen as well. When we heard the gun going off, I thought Dylan had been shot, and he thought you had. When he stood up, I was distracted enough that I was shot by a stray bullet from one of Caitlynne's sharpshooters. That's how I had been shot in the shoulder."

"Roy didn't shoot you?" He shook his head. "But how did Reed get by the shooter without getting hurt too? I mean, he was outside with the rest of them, right?"

He hadn't figured that out either and told her so. And Reed said that maybe because he'd been outside they had seen him. It didn't matter. They were all safe and sound.

"And Anita? How did I kill her?" He knew this was the part that she'd been having the nightmares about. He'd heard her screaming for Anita to back down and she would live, but in reality she'd only killed her because she had gone for him.

"You had been trying to get Khan to get us out and then you killed Roy. That was over within seconds. Anthony had been shot in the belly, but with proper medical care, he would have lived long enough to go to prison, but Anita had picked up his gun and put it right on his forehead and pulled the trigger. She killed her father just like that. But I think it was the screaming and gleeful dancing about that her daddy was dead and that she was going to be very wealthy that got you. You snarled at her, and when she turned the gun towards you, I think…. I don't really know what happened. You must have disappeared for her, because she began screaming again, screaming your name and that you were going to die."

He waited, seeing that she remembered. When she stood up and began putting the salad fixings away, he reached for her and pulled her into his arms. She seemed so stiff and cold that he knew she had to say it.

"I stood behind her as plain old Jonny and I broke her neck. I reached up and grabbed her chin and head and…. It came off in my hands. Her head did. I tore her head from her shoulders and killed her." When her arms wrapped around him, he held her. "I killed two people who richly deserved it, but I killed them all the same."

"Yes, you did. And had you not, Dylan would be dead, as well as Reed and the rest of us. When Anita couldn't find you, she started shooting around the room. Dylan was hit in the shoulder, as I had been, but she was going for him while he was down. Had you not done what you did, she would have killed him."

They finished the kitchen and went into the living room. As they sat and watched a program that neither of them seemed to be interested in, he watched her. She looked to be about a million miles away. When she turned to him, he smiled at her.

"I want to go back and work for you. You said that Mia decided not to come back, and I don't know how to be idle. Do you think you could stand that?" He nodded and grinned. "There will be no sex during working hours."

He pouted at her. When she laughed, he pulled her onto to his lap and held her there. He started to tickle her and realized with a start that she was extremely ticklish. Tickling her lasted until his phone rang.

"I wanted to know if you guys can come over tomorrow for a meeting." He raised his brow at Khan's tone. "I talked to Mom and Dad about the house, and they're none too happy with me right now. They are saying that I paid the guy who came out and looked at the house foundation to say that it was too bad and that they'd be better off dozing the house rather than try to rebuild."

"And what will the meeting be about? How to string you up? Or is it something to do with you being buried under the new foundation and we visit you on weekends?" Khan growled, and he laughed. "I told you this was going to happen."

"I know that. Don't you think I know what you said and everyone else said? But I had hoped that it would be okay for a few more years. Something more than his condemning the fucking house. And now she wants to move to a retirement home across the state, with Dad and her coming to see us once in awhile."

"Shit." Khan agreed. "And the meeting? What is this going to be about, because they are not moving across town?"

"To see which one we'd like to put them in." Khan sounded like he was having his heart ripped out of him. And Marc felt that his was as well. He didn't want them to move and told Khan that they'd be there to help convince them not to leave.

He told Jonny what they had to do, and she sat down with him on the couch. He loved his parents and couldn't imagine life without them just down the street. He started telling Jonny about Christmases in the old house, and big holiday dinners with everyone eating too much.

"Maybe my parents can talk to them." He looked at her. "They could give them some insight on what it's like not seeing me for a long time. In the meantime, I'm going to work on that thing with your dad. I can't let him get away without making his happy ass pay."

He'd forgotten about that. Jonny had been planning this for weeks, and everyone was on board, even their mom. Then she told him what was going to happen, and he started feeling pretty good. They were going to take his happy ass down. But first….

"I was thinking that you coming to work for me is a good idea. It'll give us more time together, and we can solve more cases if I'm actually at work and not wanting to be here with you. I've sort of neglected my business of late."

"No shit. But I've loved being with you. And we sort of had other things to take care of around here." He nodded. "When can I start? I have some really cool clothes I want to be able to wear."

"About that. You were a bad girl at the shop. And do you remember what I promised you?" Her eyes darkened, and she nodded. "I've been shopping online for things for toys for me to punish you with."

"I saw the package on your desk. I had to move it so the new cook and his wife didn't see it." She lay back on the couch and looked at him. "Are you going to tell me what it is?"

"No. I'm going to show you by using it. I think you'll enjoy it." She nodded at him, and he stood up. "But you need to go up to the bedroom and get it for me. And when you come back down, I want you naked."

He told her where to find it and walked to the fireplace when she left. Stoking up the fire, he turned off the television and then lit some candles. By the time she returned, he was standing in only his boxers and the room was set.

Marc knew nothing about sex toys. He'd been with a couple of women who had used them, and had gone on that little experience. He had thought for all of one second of asking for help, but knew that any one of his family members he asked would give him shit. He just wanted to please his mate. And looking at her now, standing there gloriously naked, he marveled that she was all his.

"I thought you would have opened it." He shook his head. "What if it's…I don't know, not right?"

"Are you excited?" She nodded. "Then it's just what I expected. Come here, please. I want to see you when you open it."

Marc handed her his knife and watched her open the tape. She was moving slowly, peeling the tape back and then opening the four corners gently. He didn't want her to hurry more than he wanted her to rip it open and take it out. When she did finally get the box opened, there was a second box inside among the plastic bubble wrap.

She took it out of the packaging and held the big pink dildo in her hand. "It's huge. Almost as big as you are."

He grinned at her. "Just what a man wants to hear. It's supposed to be fully charged and ready for your pleasure."

He asked her to sit down on the couch and he sat in front of her. Neither of them seemed all that sure of where to begin. It was different to play with one of these when it was someone you loved, he realized. Taking the plastic cover off, he cleaned it and turned it on.

Marc watched her face as he moved it over her to the apex of her thighs. She moaned when it moved over her pelvis, and again when he brushed it over her hip. This was going to be better than he thought.

"Open for me. Let me see how much you're enjoying this." When she spread her legs, he pulled her to the edge of the couch seat. She was so wet already that he wanted to taste her. Leaning down, he licked her from gate to clit and sat up to look at her again.

"You can't come. Not yet anyway. I want to have my fill of you, and then I might let you. And no touching, me or yourself." She nodded and put her hands up over the back of the couch. Her breasts tightened, and her nipples became hard stones. Sitting up, he took one peak into his mouth and nibbled on it until she rubbed her foot over his cock. He looked down at her.

"That's not touching you. That's rubbing you. Are you saying you don't like it?" He pulled her foot off him and set it on the floor. "You're going to get payback, you know that, right?"

"Christ, I hope so. Now behave so I can explore you. You're always in such a hurry, and I can't look." Marc worried and chewed on her other nipple until it was pink from his teeth. "Next thing I want to get is some nipple rings. The thought of making these beauties ache from them makes me want to find an Internet connection right now."

Her moan had him moving down her body, biting little hurts here and there, and licking them better. By the time he got to her navel, she was panting, and so was he. Making her suffer was having a direct effect on him. He swirled his tongue into her belly button as he moved the dildo over her again.

She was so wet when he sat between her legs again that he drank from her again, careful this time not to touch her clit. He moved the vibrator slowly in and out of her, going only an inch deep. It was enough for him to feel it vibrate against his cheek as he joined it inside of her. Lifting his head, he moved it deeper into her and pulled it out over and over again as she moved her hips in time to it.

"Marc, please. Please." He slid his fingers under her ass and watched her face. He rubbed his thumb hard over her tight muscles with her juices, and when she moaned the next time, he pressed inside of her. She screamed out her climax. Leaning in, he took her clit into his mouth and suckled until she came twice more. Moving the vibrator, he tore off his boxers, jerked her off the couch, and impaled her over him.

Her body bowed with her next climax, and he rolled them to the floor. As soon as her back touched the rug, he felt her legs tangle around his body and her ankles lock around his hips. His cock felt as if it were about to explode, and he leaned down and took her mouth in a quick, hard kiss

"You came." Her head moved in denial. "You did. And I loved it. Come for me again, love. Come so I can fill you with my seed and mark you as mine for all time."

He licked along her throat to her pounding pulse. He wanted to take her there, bite her so that his mark, the imprint of his teeth, would be where he could see it. Moving in and out of her, he felt her tighten around him. When he scraped his teeth along her vein, she curled her nails into his shoulders, pulling him to her. When she screamed again, her entire body gripping him, he sank his teeth into her flesh and felt his cock empty in her as his body took her over and over.

His bite wasn't finished, and he tore at her skin. His canines dropped, and he knew that his cat was taking his due. As soon as her blood filled his mouth, he jerked his head and tore deeper, knowing that he was leaving a scar that would be there for all time.

When she went limp beneath him, he lifted his head from her throat and licked the wound. It would heal very quickly, and he couldn't wait. Watching her face for any signs that she was in pain, he lifted himself from her and picked her up.

Taking her to their bedroom, he laid her gently on the bed. Covering her up, he kissed her and smiled when she did. Rolling to her side, he left her to close up the house.

He was nearly to the living room again when he heard his phone ringing. He answered Khan's call as he was putting out the candles.

"You do know that you're supposed to ask for permission before you mark her like that, don't you?" He asked him then. "Not the way it works, but you have my permission."

"Thank you. And I didn't do it on purpose. Well I did, but it wasn't planned. I didn't realize you could feel that."

"Neither did I. But then we're all new to this mating business." Khan was quiet as Marc took his clothes to the laundry room and set the alarm. "She hasn't pledged to me yet."

"I know. And when she does it tomorrow, be surprised, will you? Oh, and this thing with Dad is going down tomorrow. She has it all worked out with you guys, right?"

"Yes." Khan laughed. "She's sort of vindictive. Remind me never to piss her off. And Monica said to tell you that she has something for Jonny from Jack. She won't tell me what it is."

He sat down on the couch after finding a robe in the laundry room. "She asked me about what happened. I told her everything."

"Good. Now she can heal. Do you think she's going to be okay with this thing tomorrow after what happened?"

He didn't know and told Khan that. "I'm thinking that getting back at Dad will be great for her. I know it will be for me."

Khan agreed and after a few more words, they hung up. Marc was crawling into bed with Jonny when she spoke to him. He nearly went back downstairs.

"I want you to order one of those rings that go on my clit too. I think that would be fun."

CHAPTER 18

"I don't want you to move away." Everyone looked at Jonny, and she flushed. "Look, this is really stupid. You had to know that your house was falling into the basement. The guy said that it had been eroding for over fifty years. Who doesn't notice that their house is eroding? I think even I would."

"We raised our children there," Corrine snapped at her. Not that Jonny didn't blame her. She'd been getting more and more upset as the night went on. These people just seemed to like to bicker.

"And they want to give you something in return, and you got your feelings hurt and now you want to run away." Corrine stared at her, but George hopped out of his chair and stamped to her.

Jonny stood, too, and let a little of her cat go. He was bigger and much larger, but she wasn't going to back down. Not anymore. Not from anyone. He stopped and looked at Marc, who growled low.

"Sit down, George. She's right." George turned to his wife and started to speak, but she stopped him. "I am hurt. A great deal. And we did know the house was falling down. Just last summer you told me you didn't think it was going to last another winter. But it did and now…."

"Now what, Mom?" Marc asked her. "Now what? You'll need to tell us or none of us is going to be happy with this."

"Now you're all finding mates and you don't need us." Jonny snorted and she glared at her. "You do that a great deal when you have something to say. You've had no problems speaking your mind all evening, just say it."

"You thinking they don't need you is just stupid. Christ, woman, if they don't, we women certainly do. I can't make a frigging pancake, much less flip one. And I don't know how many times I've heard Monica say she was going to ask you for advice on something. Even Caitlynne goes to you for help. And Jack? That woman practically lives on your front porch." She looked at George. "And you. You're needed for your sage advice as well. Not that I will believe a single word that comes out of your mouth, but there you have it."

George grinned, then flushed when she winked at him. That man was going to pay. She wanted this settled and then to move on to the more important fun of the evening. Even Corrine was in on this thing.

"He wants me to have a new home." Corrine glared at Khan as she spoke. "What on earth am I to do with a new home, I ask you? I can barely keep the one I had."

"Yeah, well hire someone to help you. I had to, you made me." Corrine opened her mouth and Jonny snorted again. "I didn't even get to hang around tonight and have some of his…some…. I don't know what it was, but it sounded good. And there is not one speck of dust or any dirty clothes anywhere in the house. Mrs. Cable had it cleaned and shining before I got my lunch finished. And you should have tasted that chicken thing he made for me. To die for."

"Mom, I think what she's trying to tell you is to let us build you and Dad a new home and stay here with us." Marc put his hand over her mouth before she could tell them the dinner tonight was going to be beef bourguignon. "She'll behave if you stay."

Corrine smiled at him, and she looked at George, who nodded. "We'll stay. And let you build us a house, but we all know that she won't behave. We wouldn't have it any other way. She's just too rotten to even try."

Jonny wasn't sure if she had just been insulted or not, but let it go. They were staying and that was the end of it. She didn't even have to ask her parents to get involved. They were having too much fun buying things for their new house with the check they'd received.

It had been more than she'd ever thought it would be, nearly eight million dollars. When she'd asked Marc about it, he'd told her that the government gave them a percentage of what Roy and the others had cost them over the years. And the reward for any information on the capture and conviction of Anthony Kidd had been five million alone. She'd looked it up. That part had been right, but she never could find anything on the other part.

She looked up when Khan sat next to her. "You did that well. I owe you. I would have just demanded and yelled."

"You always yell and demand. You rarely get things to be the way you want them, but you still do it. The only person you don't yell at is Monica. I think you're afraid of her." Khan looked around and saw Monica wasn't in the room and told her he was, a little. "Good. She's a little meaner than you are in a sneaky sort of nice person sort of way."

She looked at Marc, who winked at her. She'd told him that she was going to pledge to Khan today, but was a little nervous about it. Marc had told her what he'd be able to do for her, and she thought that him finding her at any cost and being able to bring her cat and stuff was okay, but she didn't want him to have access to her noodle. There had been enough probing around in her head. She looked at the doorway just as Walker came in, and when he nodded, she looked at Khan.

"Show time. You ready?" He nodded and took a deep breath. She knew he wasn't thrilled about his part. He was sort of the catalyst to the whole thing to making it work. She watched him as he struggled to do his job.

When he wrapped his arm around her, she smiled at him. She didn't even have to look at Marc to know that he was coming toward them. As was Jack. They both stood before them about the same time, and then Jack reached up and wrapped her arms around Marc in a sort of attempt to stop him from hurting Khan. Oh boy, the fun was beginning.

"Let him go." She stood just as Khan did. "I said to let my mate go. If you don't back off now, it's within my rights to kill you."

George started toward them, worry on his face. Corrine stepped out of the room. Her part was to come later. When Jack slapped her, Jonny lunged, and it was a free for all.

~~~

Khan had tried his best to hold his own with the two women. They were having fun, too much as far as he was concerned. He stood on the deck and watched the two of them go at each other. His dad and Marc stood to his right, Dylan to his left.
~~~

"Aren't you going to do something? One of them is going to get killed. Then what the hell are you going to do?" Khan looked at his dad. "Do something, you're the leader."

"Neither of them have pledged to me. I can't do anything, their mates have to. Besides, this is sort of your fault. You've been telling Jonny for weeks that she would have to kill anyone who touched her mate. If one of them is killed, it's your fault."

"Good God, I was kidding with her. She certainly didn't take me seriously, did she?" Khan nodded to the women in the yard still snapping and fighting each other. "Oh my. What have I done?"

Dylan leapt over the railing as soon as Jonny drew blood from Jack. It wasn't really anything more than a tiny baggy of blood that Walker had taken from her that morning. No one was really going to get hurt doing this, but the scent stirred his blood as well. As soon as Dylan had grabbed Jonny, Marc shifted and jumped into the fray. They were moving so quickly it was hard to tell who was who, other than the males were bigger than the females, and Jack and Jonny were fighting better.

Dylan lunged at Marc just as he nipped at Jack. Khan was pretty sure that Jack could have handled him on her own, but that wasn't the plan. The whole thing was going just as she'd planned right down to his mom coming out and telling someone to stop it. Then he watched in pretend horror as Jonny bit at Jack's throat and tore it away. While she lay there "dying," Dylan knocked Marc down and "snapped" his neck.

Khan glanced to the garage where Reed was doing the sound effects and winced. That had been as loud as a fucking gun going off, and he saw that the limb that he'd used for the bones breaking were huge. The kid never did a damned thing in moderation. His dad sat down hard on the step as Dylan and Jonny stood over their victims.

Walker came out of the house and ran to them. He had his bag with him, and Caitlynne was right behind him. The two of them looked up on the deck and shook their heads.

Khan looked at his dad when he started to clap his hands. He looked at Jonny, then back at him. His dad started laughing and was soon leaning back on the stairs to catch his breath. Marc and Jack sat up, knowing the gig was up.

"You didn't really expect me to believe this, did you?" Khan looked at his mom, who shook her head. "No, no she didn't tell me. I figured it out on my own. I knew the moment that you stayed up here on the deck that it wasn't real. You should have helped them, your brothers at least, and I know for a fact that Jack pledged to you last month. I may be old, son, but I'm not stupid."

"You prick." Khan looked at Jonny as she came toward them, pulling her shirt over her nudity. "You mean old prick. You knew and you let this go on. Jack fucking bit me."

"Of course she did. You guys did an outstanding job. It was Khan's fault all around. He should have helped, and he didn't. He would have, too, but…. Damn, girl, this was a hell of a payback. But you knew I was just funning with you, right?"

Jonny walked by them and into the house. Marc followed her and mumbled "thanks, Dad" as he walked by them. His dad looked up at him, looking confused. So was Khan. He thought she would have it out with him. They both looked up at Monica when she came out of the house.

"They're leaving. They said to tell everyone goodnight." His dad stood up and looked at Monica when she started talking to him. "Jonny said if you needed anything to let her know. She said she was going to start working Monday and would speak to you about something then."

"What the hell do you mean they're leaving? We were having fun. You go and get them right now and tell that little girl to get back out here." Monica shook her head and looked to the drive when the crunch of gravel sounded. "They really left?"

"Yes. What did you expect, you old fool? That poor girl didn't know anything about us or even her own kind, and you go and stir up trouble for her. Then she tries to come up with this elaborate, beautiful plan, and you mess it up for her. Couldn't you have acted the least bit impressed?" Khan's mom smacked his dad on the shoulder. "And now look what you've done. They're gone and pissed at you again."

"But she seemed to be fine with it." His dad looked at Khan. "You knew I was just kidding. I kid around with everyone. It's what I do."

"Well, you'd better fix this or so help me I will." His mom poked his dad in the chest. "And trust me, you won't like the way I fix this."

"I'll call her right now. I'll fix this. I might have gone a little too far with her, her being a novice and all. But she did a fine job on getting you all to work together. Fine job." He pulled out his cell phone and began to search for her name. "She's the best thing for Marc. Who would have thought he'd fall so hard for a lovely girl like her? Not that I didn't think he would, it's just that I thought his heart was closed and she just went right in and opened it right up. I don't seem to have her number. Can I have it?"

"Got you." They all turned to look at Jonny, who was standing behind his dad. "See, you do like me."

His dad grabbed her then. Dropping his cell phone, he pulled her into his arms and held her. Jonny was so stunned looking that Khan nearly laughed. His dad told her he was sorry, and that he didn't just like her, he loved her. Khan then reached for his mom. She leaned her head on his shoulder and smiled up at him.

"I helped her with this part. Just in case the other didn't go as planned." Khan kissed his mom on the forehead. "She's a wonder, isn't she? I wanted to smack her earlier, but she's right. We should have known we couldn't live there forever."

"She seems to be good for all of us." He looked toward his other two brothers, who stood alone. "Do you think that their mates will be just as stubborn as ours are, or do you think they'll be more timid? I don't know if I can take another strong female in this family."

"I think that Reed's mate will take him out of his shell and bring him away from his computers and back into our lives. Not that he's not here, but he does have his head buried into some sort of electrical equipment all the time." Khan nodded.

"And Sebastian? What do you foresee in his life? A female to bring him out of his computers too? Though he's not as bad as Reed, he does tend to zone out when something electronic is brought to his attention."

They watched Sebastian hug Caitlynne when she made a comment about his shirt. It was as loud as Reed's snap had been with colors, enough to make a crayon company jealous. And where did he even get those shirts anyway? It seemed that every time he saw him he had on one that was brighter and uglier. And the last time he'd had on a suit, the shirt and tie had clashed so badly that Khan had begged him to take the tie off even though they'd been at a formal function.

"No, Sebastian's mate will be someone that won't be easily swayed by him, I think. She'll have to be strong because of his quiet reserve, Sebastian is a strong man and stronger in his ways. I think his mate will be someone that he will cherish, but she won't have it. He's the most romantic son I have, and she will probably hate it…for a time anyway."

Khan laughed and kissed his mom again. His dad was telling Jonny what a great kid she was, but still only a kid, and slapped Marc on the back. Khan walked to Jonny and kissed her cheek. She looked up at him, as serious as he had ever seen her.

"I need to pledge to you. I think it's stupid and a little on the barbaric side, but you seem to need it from me. But I want more of a reason. I'll do it, but there should be more of a reason for me to do it than because I have to." She glanced at his mom. "I want you to tell me what I'll get out of this, and not what you'll get out of it."

He thought about telling her she'd get to be a member of his family, but looked around and saw that she already was. A huge part of his family, as a matter of fact. Then he thought of something Caitlynne had told him after he'd made her pledge to him, and thought that Jonny more than likely needed the same thing.

"When Caitlynne lay dying in my arms, I had never felt more helpless or more pissed in my life. This woman had refused to pledge to me because she told me later that I had made it sound not like she was pledging anything but submitting to me. She said that all it sounded to her was that I was going to get this connection to her and that I was going to be able to call to her cat and that I was going to be able to find her if she was missing. She said that it was hard to give up what she didn't feel I deserved but had demanded of her."

"What did you tell her, Khan, just shut up and do it my way?" She snorted, a habit he was beginning to see that she was using instead of cursing at him. "I'm betting you put her into her place, didn't you?"

He laughed. "Have you met Caitlynne? The only person that put her into her place is Caitlynne. She's harder on herself than you are, and honey you are hard on yourself. But in answer to your question, no, I didn't. Well, that's not true, I did, but I amended it later. I spoke to her again after I met Monica."

"He told me that I was gaining more than he was." Caitlynne walked up beside him as she continued speaking to Jonny. "Not only did I get all the things that he'd gain from me, such as the ability to contact and call my cat, but that I'd have his heart. He said that when a person pledged to a leader of a family, they were bound to him, nothing more, just bound. But when someone pledged to him that was a mate to his brothers, they got a large chunk of his heart as well. Because they loved and cherished the most important people he knew, his blood family."

Jonny grinned at him when he flushed. Cheeky girl was going to be the death of him, he knew it. When she bent on one knee, everyone around them grew quiet, even the insects and birds. She held up her right hand and offered it to him. He realized then that she'd been reading on the old traditions.

"Khan Bowen, leader of the Bowen family and blood brother to my mate Marc Bowen, I give to you my pledge freely and willingly. I also give to you my children until such time that they can decide to pledge to you as well. I, Jonny Erma Thomas Bowen, give you all that I have to offer." She looked up at him when she had recited the words that he'd never heard said to him before. "You old softy."

He decided right then and there that he was going to make her life a living hell, then glanced over at the other three women in his life and changed his mind. If the four of them ever got together to hatch a plan to get back at him, he might not survive it. He was sure he wouldn't. They seemed to have formed their own little click, and he was afraid of it. Looking at his mated brothers as they watched the women, he was pretty sure that they had the same thought. All of them might be the stronger males in this family, but none of them were going to fuck with the women. Ever.

Khan went to his dad and hugged him. The man was a pain in the ass, and he never knew when to quit, but he was the best father he'd ever had, and told him so.

"You do know that I am your only father, right?" Khan nodded, and his dad stared. "I suppose if I asked you to explain, you'd just tell me some bull story about it being about love and all."

Khan nodded and followed his entire family into the house. He was a man who was in love. In love with life, his family, and with himself. Then he remembered what his mom had said and groaned. What the hell else could happen?

ABOUT THE AUTHOR

Kathi Barton, author of the bestselling series Force of Nature, lives in Nashport, Ohio with her husband Paul. In addition to writing full time Kathi likes to spend time with her eight grandkids, three children and three children-in-laws. She writes to relax and have fun.

Her muse, a cross between Jimmy Stewart and Hugh Jackman brings them to life for her readers in a way that has them coming back time and again for more. Her favorite genre is paranormal romance with a great deal of spice. You can visit Kathi on line and drop her an email if you'd like. She loves hearing from her fans. aaronskiss@gmail.com.

Follow Kathi on her blog:
http://kathisbartonauthor.blogspot.com/

www.ingramcontent.com/pod-product-compliance
Lightning Source LLC
LaVergne TN
LVHW090935080826
845145LV00003B/763